NO HONOR AMONG THIEVES

KATHERINE KIM

No Honor Among Thieves © 2022 Katherine Kim. All rights reserved. This book or parts thereof may not be reproduced in any form, stored in any retrieval system, or transmitted in any form by any means—electronic, mechanical, photocopy, recording, or otherwise—without prior written permission of the publisher, except as provided by United States of America copyright law. For permission requests, write to the publisher, at katherineukim@gmail.com

---

This is a work of fiction. Names, characters, places, and incidents either are the products of the author's imagination or are used fictitiously. Any resemblance to actual persons, living or dead, businesses, companies, or events is entirely coincidental.

Follow me on Instagram @katherineukim or on Facebook www.facebook.com/katherineukim

Cover by Enchanted Ink Studio

Editing by Robin J Samuels www.shadowcatediting.com

> Copyright © 2022 Katherine Kim
> All rights reserved.

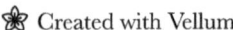 Created with Vellum

A NOTE

I have made wild and probably reckless adjustments and bent Wilmington, North Carolina to my will. I fully admit that I Made Things Up and then put them wherever I wanted to, so please, if you live there or otherwise know the place, forgive me. I am invoking my Artist's License here.

Keep up with new releases, giveaways, and other antics by joining my email community. You'll get news of releases, a free short story, updates from any shenanigans I get up to, and all sorts of things!

Otherwise you might consider looking at my Patreon page, where you will get weekly progress updates and the opportunity for advance access to short stories and novels, sometimes as I'm writing them!

1

"Give up. You're not getting away and running is only going to make things worse." Darien held his hands out in front of him, trying to calm the wild-eyed man in front of them.

Caroline braced, her hand wrapped around the grip of her fancy Taser, waiting to see the guy's reaction. They had been helping Mack and a few other agents break up a mid-level drug deal in this old warehouse area, in hopes of getting more information on the latest generation of paranormal-affecting drugs. Of course, then this guy took off running. Much too fast to be human, but clumsy since he was impaired by whatever he was on, the guy now hissed at Darien.

Vampire then. Okay.

The guy's eyes darted around wildly, searching for a way out. His gaze landed on Caroline, recognizing her as the weak point.

"Don't do it, buddy," Darien said. He took a slow step forward, almost close enough to grab the guy. "Just come along with us nice and politely, okay? We'll get you some medical attention, a solid meal. You can maybe help us out. Just don't–"

The vampire hissed again, and Caroline heard the defiance and panic in the sound. She shifted her weight in preparation. He lunged sideways, then spun to leap at Caroline. She fired her taser, the magic-electric charge stored up in it surging forth, but the man's erratic movement saved him at the last moment, the darts siding past his arm and getting tangled in his shirt. Without any other options Caroline threw herself at the man, hoping to slow him down. He plowed into her full force and she wrapped her arms around his waist. It was only a second before he shoved her away and into a plastic-wrapped pallet of boxes, but it was enough.

The fight between the two vampires was short. Without the impairment of drugs clouding Darien's judgment and dulling his abilities had no difficulty taking the other vamp down. After reading the man his rights and helping him stand up again, hands cuffed behind him with paranormal-strength restraints, Darien turned to Caroline. She groaned at the expression on his face.

"You okay, Sunshine?" he asked.

"Yeah, I'm fine," she said with a shrug. "A few bruises. I've had worse. He was getting away and my damn taser missed."

"I'll put it on the list of things to tell Peaches for your next training session." Darien shook his head. "I hate when they fight back."

Caroline sighed. The life of a Federal Paranormal Activities Agency intern involved a lot more combat training than she had expected when she started.

Caroline growled at her computer screen and wished these forms would fill themselves out. She wasn't even a real agent yet, just an intern! *She* didn't arrest the guy! Sure, she had flung herself in his way when he tried to escape Darien and got a few bruises for it, but come on. They were only bruises, it's not like she bled or anything. She had suffered through much worse. But no, Chief Point was making her fill out an incident report. Again.

"You've definitely been hanging out with the shifters, Sunshine," Darien said as he put a coffee mug on her desk. "That was a respectable growl."

"Stupid incident report," she grumbled. "Why is it my fault that the guy ran into me? Point should make *him* fill out a report!"

Darien laughed and sat in his chair at the desk facing hers. A bit taller than she was, fit, with scruffy dark hair and eyes like a hot cup of cocoa on a snow day, Darien had inspired more than one of her fellow students to cast jealous glares her way in the lecture halls.

It made Caroline laugh, though. She thought of him more like the most irritating honorary brother a girl could have, much to her mother's disappointment. At least, he was a brother until they were facing down criminal crazies who wanted them both dead. Then Darien was a seriously badass vampire and she was very glad was on her side.

"I'd guess it's because you manage to get yourself sent to the infirmary at least once a month? And because you're the one who chose to jump in front of a fleeing suspect who was high as a kite. I could have caught him if he'd gotten to the door."

"You're supposed to be supportive!" Caroline whined and slumped over her keyboard. "And how am I supposed to be an effective agent if I let my partner do all the hard work?"

Darien laughed again.

"Filling out an incident report again, huh?"

Caroline jumped at the comment from right behind her. She heard equal measures of sympathy and amusement in Greg's voice as the shifter leaned over her shoulder. Damn silet ninja cat.

"Man, that's impressive. Not even I have to fill out this many, and I've got to do one for every time I shift on the job!"

"Wait, really?" Caroline perked up.

"Yep." The big blond man wasn't even looking at her. He was watching the soft stress balls he juggled whirl through the air. "The grand poobahs of bureaucracy love their forms. Got to make sure I didn't endanger the secrecy of the paranormal world on a whim, you know."

He grinned as he said it. Greg was another one that got her glared at on campus and another honorary brother with not a spark of romantic tension between them. Didn't seem to matter to her fellow students at the university, though.

He looked like he should be an underwear model and acted like he was an excited toddler half the time, but she was always happy to have him watching her back when she was in a pinch. In either his human form or as the world's only known manticore, the man could be lethal. He was a lot more settled now since they had rescued him and Spark from the megalomaniac that kidnapped them both.

The psycho had wanted to use them to raise an army of manticores to take over the world—Greg because he was a manticore and Spark because he was the Aldebrand's own son. The man seemed to think that if his army was genetically related to him they would be more subservient. I mean, had he met Spark?

Caroline could not even make all that up. She glanced back at her computer screen.

"You need to stop throwing yourself into trouble, kitten," Greg continued. "I mean, I know I'm one to talk, but my bulk has more stopping power than yours does."

"True, but I still slowed him down plenty," Caroline snipped back. She sighed. "This is actually less fun than the paper I need to write for my history class later. Which is impressive." Darien and Greg both cracked up at that.

"Ugh,"she grunted and turned back to her keyboard. The dumb form was almost finished if she were being honest.

"Hey, your spring break's coming up soon, isn't it?" Greg asked.

"It is. I have all next week off. I have the paper for history and one test, then freedom!"

Not that she was planning to do anything other than sleep in and get some work done on the last projects of the semester. Point had even given her the week off—insisted she take the vacation time—in case she wanted to go home and see her folks, but she didn't really. She had a trip planned for the summer, but the small town felt less and less like home every time she went back. Stonehaven was home now.

Julia, her landlord-slash-roommate had even said that she didn't need to move out when she graduated in a few years. Honestly, now that she had stopped trying to set Caroline up with all her very strange friends, Julia was pretty cool. Now if Caroline could just get her mom to lay off her love life—or lack of one—she'd be pretty content with her life.

She typed the last words into the form and hit submit

before also hitting print since Point had very explicitly demanded a copy on his desk before she left today. Darien and Greg were discussing Greg's current case, and the rest of the office clattered on in its merry governmental way.

Human mages, as well as elves, vampires, shifters, and various other types of paranormals, wandered around holding files or joking around on the way to the break room.

"Greg! Any updates?" Point called from his office door. The troll was looking damn near cheerful today, his needle-like teeth peeking out from the occasional grin, which was rare enough since he took the Section Chief position almost two years ago now.

Caroline grinned, thinking about how fast the troll settled into the job after the disastrous mess that had started her involvement with the FPAA and the wider paranormal world. She still regretted that she and Darien had left the old Chief alive, but it had been extremely satisfying to watch him stand trial for treason.

After that Point go the promotion and went through the Stonehaven office with a fine-toothed comb, brought Caroline herself in as an intern-slash-trainee-agent, and basically lived up to the grumpy police chief image, especially when there was a big case. There hadn't been any major cases for them to worry about in the past few months since the Aldebrand case wrapped up, and everyone was breathing easier.

Since they dealt with Aldebrand it had been relatively calm. Even the Elf Supremacists had been quiet, keeping their vitriol confined to internet chat rooms and a couple of rallies in DC.

"I sent in my latest report a few minutes ago, but nothing particularly helpful. We're waiting on Ollie's test results and Mack's interrogation," Greg called back.

"Great, keep me posted," Point answered :Caroline! I want you helping out in interrogation three in twenty minutes!" He added with a grumble. His voice was smoother today, like river stones, and turned to head off to the break room. Probably to terrify the poor coffee machine into producing another pot of coffee strong enough to fuel a vehicle.

"He's looking less gray around the edges lately," Caroline commented.

"Yeah. I guess knowing that one of your agents is less likely to be hunted down as a lab specimen can be a real stress relief," Darien agreed.

"Hey! It's not like I asked for that psycho to hunt me down!" Greg grumbled.

"We never said you did." Caroline reached out to squeeze his arm now that he had stopped juggling the stress balls. "We're all just glad that Lucas was able to track you down and help figure out who had you."

"Yeah, and that he was willing to work with Shakes to trace all of Aldebrand's connections and crazy schemes after he'd gotten some rest. Shakes is *still* sorting it all out, but at least it's not time-sensitive anymore." Darien sighed and stretched in his chair. "That guy had his fingers in everything."

"Yeah. I used to think that movie-style megalomaniac supervillains were made up by Hollywood," Caroline agreed.

"Or comic books!" Greg added "But yeah. The guy was crazy. From what Spark says, he was always a little nuts, but I guess sometime between losing me and Spark, then getting involved with the Elf Supremacists, even if it was just to manipulate them, the guy lost his hold on reality."

"Still. I mean, I'd met some ego-driven crazies before that," Caroline said, then fake coughed "Ex-Chief Beckett"

"Ugh, ego and bigotry. What a delightful combination," Darien groaned. He had been the one most affected by that adventure, getting set up to be beaten and murdered by his ex-boss simply because Darien was a vampire. He grinned over at Caroline. "At least we got you out of that particular mess."

"And now I have to fill out an endless stream of incident reports. Yay," Caroline groaned. Darien and Greg chuckled, but neither offered to help.

2

Caroline stepped out of the observation room and into the hallway. Mack stepped out of the interrogation room and grinned at her.

"Never leave, C. My interrogations have never been so fast or so productive," he said.

She laughed. "I'm glad my weird, unexplainable skill is good for something at least. It got me in more trouble when I was a kid. Just being a human lie detector is not so bad. Accidentally hearing all sorts of things nobody actually said out loud? Not so great."

"I can just bet!" he said. "Hard to keep birthday presents secret when you can pick the information out of their 'good morning,' huh?"

"God," Caroline groaned. "When I was about five, I remember my aunt came over with my cousins to hang out. Mom was making some sort of small talk, and when my aunt answered, I could hear that she was stressed about what everyone would think when she divorced her husband, and I asked her why she wanted to beat up my uncle."

"Oh shit!"

"Yeah, it was a tough month," she agreed.

Mack cracked up and waved as he headed the other way down the hall.

Caroline chuckled and headed back to her desk. Being what Mitch, one of the lab mages, called empath-adjacent was not the easiest way to grow up. It warmed her heart to know that she had finally found someplace to use her odd ability. He had grilled her for months when she started her internship, trying to figure out where it came from and what its limits were, with only limited results. The best that anyone could figure out was that someone in Caroline's family had a secret affair with a paranormal and passed those magical genetics down the line until something in Caroline activated them.

Mitch had a long-winded explanation for his theory of why she could pick up the odd bit of information just from hearing someone speak, but hadn't been able to help her focus her odd skill. And as much as Caroline wished she could control it—seek out particular information from a suspect or turn it off entirely- it was no good. The only really reliable aspect of her talent was the ability to tell when someone was lying. It was a handy trick during interviews and interrogations.

Back at her desk she shuffled a few files around and cleared up some paperwork, but she was out of urgent tasks for the day and was now just trying to pass time. She still had a little over two hours until she could go home. A ping on her phone had her glancing over at it, but it was only a reminder of her paper's upcoming due date.

"Text from your technomage?" Darien asked. He aimed a rubber band at her and let it fly, hitting her square in the chest. She glared at him—her rubber band shooting skills were nonexistent so she couldn't even retaliate. Darien grinned, unrepentant.

"No, in fact. It was a reminder that I should go home and work on my paper after work," she answered. "It's the last big thing between me and spring break. I mean, if you don't count my math midterm, which I don't. I've got that one in the bag."

Darien raised an eyebrow at her. "Not even going to study?"

"Nah," Caroline said. "I'll review my notes and the textbook and do some basic review, but this semester has been pretty easy for me. I don't know, it just makes sense to me."

"And your paper doesn't?"

"Eh, it does. And it's interesting stuff, I just don't really have the motivation to write about it. I'd much rather read about it. Or watch another documentary on the weird but true history of enchantments," she said. Caroline grinned, thinking of the way-too-bingeable show she streamed last weekend.

"That show Lucas turned you on to is going to rot your brain," Darien said, reading her mind. "And apparently it will also cost you a term paper."

Caroline scrunched up her face and stuck out her tongue. Very mature, she knew, but who cared? She was only twenty, after all, and it was only Darien.

"Where is our favorite pain in the butt? He helped Spark track down the money in that fraud case and I haven't heard from him since. That was what, a month ago now?" Darien asked.

Caroline started to answer, but then stopped and really thought about it. "Not sure, now that you've mentioned it. He sent me that link to the weird enchantments show and I think that was the last I heard from him. A little over a week, I guess?"

"I wonder what trouble he's getting into now? He drops off the face of the earth, then turns up a few weeks later with some terrible cover story of a vacation or helping a friend move or something. Last time he did this, there was a huge news story about a crate full of missing artifacts being returned to the Egyptian Antiquities people at the same time as a suspiciously convenient arrest was made by the FBI regarding illegal artifact trading in California."

None of them had any doubts that Lucas was using slightly less-than-legal means to handle certain problems. What none of them could figure out was how he picked what problems to fix and what he got out of it. Darien assumed he got some kind of cut, but Caroline didn't think so.

It wouldn't make sense, would it? Stealing something to anonymously return it to the rightful owner couldn't come with a huge commission fee.

"Well, I guess we'll find out when he gets back. Assuming he's actually gone anywhere. He might just be hanging out at home. Maybe he's got the flu. Who knows. I'll text him though, see if he needs a wellness check or something."

Darien snorted. "I don't like that I like the guy. I also think it would take more than a bowl of chicken soup to fix what's wrong with him."

Caroline sent him another glare. "Don't be a jerk." She picked up her phone and started typing.

Caroline: *Hey. Just checking in. We haven't heard from you in a few minutes so we were wondering what you're up to. Please don't cause any international incidents.*

She put her phone back on the desk and sighed. "Well, that's about all we can do unless you want Shakes to use

FPAA resources to try to track him down. And considering he's one of the few technomages in the world, I don't think Shakes would have a lot of luck if Lucas didn't want to be found, no matter how good Shakes is."

Lucas could get around any computer or program, and not even the best that the Federal Paranormal Activities Agency could throw at him would defeat his magic. It was like bringing a steel knife to a laser sword fight.

"Doesn't it bug you that he just goes off and does whatever? He won't talk about it. What if he's up to something?" Darien frowned.

Caroline rolled her eyes. "We know he's up to something. The question, really, is what? Remember how we met? He was investigating the disappearance of a student and got all tangled up in that human trafficking case and ended up being such a huge help. Because he was up to something."

"He's not a private investigator, though, Caroline," he said. "He shouldn't be investigating anything."

Caroline smirked at her friend. "And that's probably why he doesn't talk to us about it."

"What he should do is just get his damn license—I'd help him myself—then he should tell us when he has a case that would involve him disappearing for any period of time," Darien grumbled back at her.

"We're his friends. Hell, he's damn near family for all the time he's spent here. I don't think anyone here is such an aggressive rule-follower that they would arrest him for being slightly shady. Which he is."

Caroline hummed in thought. "So if he was involved with the antiquities bust, which likely involved going in and stealing the antiquities that were mysteriously returned, so that he could mysteriously return them, you'd look the other way?"

Darien shrugged. "If there was any evidence of his involvement, then nobody's said anything. All we know is that there was an anonymous tip plausible and convincing enough to get a warrant issued, at coincidentally the same time as a crate of Egyptian antiquities was arriving at a museum in Cairo. While Lucas happened to be doing one of his disappearing acts."

Caroline raised an eyebrow at him.

"Look, I'm not saying I think it's all a bunch of unconnected coincidences, but come on. Aside from the possible breaking and entering part, it was all perfectly legal. Or at least not illegal in a way that a halfway decent lawyer couldn't talk around," Darien said. "Going off on his own like this is dangerous. Remember that same case we met him on? Where he came damn close to getting himself captured? What would have happened if we hadn't been involved? He'd have disappeared without a trace and nobody would have known better."

"He's a technomage. I'm pretty sure that he could have managed to get away at some point. Hell, he taught me how to pick analog locks, even," she reminded him.

Darien sighed. "Caroline, I'm just worried, okay?"

She glanced at her silent phone and grimaced. She could understand that. She was getting a bit worried too.

3

Only another hour of work before she got to go home and start more work. She stepped into the break room to grab a drink and saw that Mitch was there, fussing in the corner.

"Hey, Caroline. I started some more coffee if you would like some."

"No thanks, I'm just after some water." She grabbed a bottle from the fridge and turned back to him. "Taking a few minutes away from the lab?"

Mitch groaned. "Ollie is on a rampage about that substance you all brought in from your bust. It's proving difficult to analyze for some reason. I'm not involved with that case, but Ollie is making the lab...difficult to work in."

Caroline could imagine. A frustrated eight-foot ogre could make a lot of things difficult. Even an eight-foot ogre in a lab coat.

"Aren't you on your spring break now?" he asked, returning to the pot as it finished gurgling the last of the coffee into the carafe.

"Next week. I'm only here today because my history

professor got sick. I still have to turn in my paper though, assuming I get the thing finished." She slumped into a chair at one of the long tables and sighed. "I'm a little stuck."

"What's it about?"

"The history of controlled enchantments in law enforcement. I'm supposed to discuss the advancements in regulation and storage of dangerous enchanted objects." Caroline sighed. "The subject is interesting, but I just can't seem to get motivated about it."

Mitch chuckled. "Considering your activities this morning, you're perhaps more practical in your concerns than theoretical."

Caroline grinned. "I suppose you're right."

"I could show you our vault, if that would spur you on somewhat?" Mitch said before sipping his coffee. "There's also a central storage facility not too far from here. A little over an hour drive into the mountains."

"You'd show me the vault?" Caroline sat up in her chair and gaped at him. She had never been allowed near that area of the facility. It was under the parking garage and very secure.

Mitch chuckled. "I'd have to check with Point first, but I don't see why not."

Caroline groaned. "I may never get to see it, then."

Mitch chuckled. "He's not that irritable."

"And I am more of a hands-on practical learner. Reading things in books and listening to lectures is fine, but if I really want it to stick, I have to do it. Or, you know, see it, I guess."

Mitch nodded. "Well, our vault isn't as large or impressive as the central storage facility, but it's quite respectable."

"I bet! Can you tell me about it?" Caroline leaned

forward. This was much more interesting than either paperwork or, well, writing papers.

"Well, safe handling can vary widely depending on the object in question, as well as the enchantment. A gun enchanted to make a flatulence sound when fired is considered a dangerous enchantment just as readily as a charm that could suppress the human immune system, but they both need to be handled in different manners."

"That is...oddly specific," Caroline said.

"Indeed," Mitch said, giving her a flat look over his glasses. "Both are currently stored in the vault. The charm is due to be transferred to the central facility soon now that the case has been ruled on and the object is no longer needed on site. After a period of twenty years, the enchantment will be disassembled and the charm may be sold at auction. The gun, however, may stay enchanted or not in the end, depending on who is making the ruling, but as the case it is involved in is ongoing I cannot speak to the timeline or the likely outcome."

"I kind of love it when you get all stuffy and professorial." Caroline grinned. "So what makes our vault so special? How's it different from, say, a museum or a private collection?"

"Well, for one thing, private"–Mitch coughed lightly–"collectors are not always concerned with either preservation or safety. That gun we have in the vault? It was used, repeatedly, which is why it is in our vault now. The charm was, as far as we know, only used once," Mitch said with a sigh.

Caroline grimaced. Right. They only got hold of these interesting things due to active use, which kind of dulled the excitement over the cool stuff.

"And museums often take steps to deactivate any potentially harmful enchantments while keeping as much of both the object and the enchantment intact as possible, to ensure continuity of the historical and cultural record," Mitch continued. "Here, we are primarily concerned with containing or deactivating the enchantments and the possible danger to the public rather than any sort of preservation or curation."

Caroline nodded. "I did think it was a bit odd back in that first case I worked, you remember? I mean, I would consider a bomb that could affect the weather to be pretty dangerous, even in as limited an area as it was intended to, and it was just sitting there in the display case."

Mitch nodded. "Exactly. Although the man in charge there was less concerned about keeping the historical record intact than he was with making it easy for thieves who paid him to stroll in and take whatever they wished to. He certainly wasn't particularly concerned with safety. That said, by and large museums and archival institutions try to evaluate the possible danger of any item they acquire, then take steps to ensure the safe storage and handling of the item in question. It isn't much different than any non-enchanted objects in that sense."

Mitch refilled his mug and came to sit at the table. "Now, that said, it is often more akin to handling a toxic substance. One must take care not to touch the item, or accidentally activate the enchantment. The horn was activated by playing it, for example. The charm downstairs simply needed to be worn, and considering it is the sort of item that a young woman would be inclined to wear often, it was particularly effective. She was quite fortunate that her friend was an accomplished witch and noticed immediately that there was something afoot."

"Damn," Caroline muttered. "How do you figure out how an enchantment is active? How do you break the enchantment?"

"Enchantment breaking is, itself, a complicated process and often takes magic users some time to learn to do effectively and well. Essentially, one must first determine the flow of magic energies, then..." Mitch sighed and frowned quietly for a moment. "It is a bit like trying to determine the path of circuitry in a bomb where you can only see part of the wires. You must be careful not to make matters worse by accident. Does that make sense? I don't often have to explain it to someone that is not a practicing mage."

Caroline grinned. "Yeah, I got it. So, breaking dangerous enchantments is a bit like bomb disposal. I guess it makes sense why museums don't do it a lot then. It must get expensive to keep someone on staff with those skills."

"Indeed. Security firms and, well, the FPAA, tend to have more attractive salary and benefit packages than museums. Unfortunate, but there it is," Mitch said with a shrug. "So, often when a museum or scholarly institution acquires an object that needs to be handled, they call us or a private security firm that is licensed for hazardous enchantment breaking. Here, however, as I said, we often can't do anything but store the item until the case is over, so we must take different steps to contain the danger. It's a surprisingly analog system." He chuckled.

Caroline blinked now. "Analog?"

"Indeed. Unusual in today's digital world, but magic and technology have some sort of mutual antipathy. If we could discover a way to encase a dangerous enchantment in circuitry we could do that, but unfortunately all the solutions of that type that we have come up with are either far too bulky to make them practical for either museums or law enforcement, or entirely enclose the object, thus shielding it from view. Also, given the wildy variable size and shape requirements for such a storage system, it becomes financially inefficient."

"But...Lucas is a technomage. Literally all his magic is technology-based," Caroline said, frowning deeply. "Well, I guess not all of it, but still. He handles enchanted stuff all the time, and does magic stuff on the internet and.. um... stuff."

Mitch leaned forward and his eyes glittered. "I know! That is one reason I am so fascinated by him! I have had him perform several simple tasks as slowly as he can while I observed, and the flow of magic was entirely unlike anything I have seen before! He turned on a lamp from across the room and I could have written an entire series of articles on that action alone! If it wouldn't be dangerous for him, and anyone else like him, I would publish in a heartbeat. Sadly, even if we used a pseudonym, these days someone would discover who the subject was."

Mitch's shoulders slumped now and his expression grew grim. "We have had enough experience in this very office with leaks to make me more than concerned about security. I know that Point has instituted extra security measures in the vault, the lab, and the IT suite. Both technological and magical scans and so on."

Caroline groaned. "I know. I had to have my aura scanned three times just so I could keep my lab access."

Mitch chuckled again, his good humor restored. "You're another somewhat special case, Caroline. Not as rare as Lucas, but it's not often we can't sort out what type of magic runs in a person's blood." He sat back and finished off his coffee. "Lucas seems to be a new evolution in human magical ability, as well as in magic at large. And you? The few cases similar to yours were easily enough sorted out by finding rumors or family stories of affairs with the paranormal, one way or another. But your family has been frustratingly straightforward in their scandals."

"So sorry my family tree couldn't titillate you." Caroline grinned.

"I live for intellectual gossip." Mitch winked back, his professor hat off now that the conversation had moved on from his lecture.

"So tell me what our magical anomaly is up to. I haven't seen Lucas around recently. Should we be warning one of the other offices about an incoming case?"

Caroline frowned again and pulled out her phone, which remained silent.

"I wish I knew, Mitch."

4

"Am I trudging? I feel like I'm trudging," Caroline groaned.

Beside her Spark laughed. "I think you're mostly just whining. It's not that far. Your apartment is like, two blocks from here, then it's all spring break for you. I still have a class in the morning."

Caroline grinned. Spark was pretty cool. He was a few years older than she was and just starting college thanks to his complicated history, which involved a megalomaniacal father bent on world domination via kidnapping. Fortunately, the guy was now awaiting trial on so many charges that Caroline couldn't even count them all, and Spark was free to finally pursue his own dreams and goals. Most of which seemed to involve playing guitar and hanging out with Greg, and when he was at school, with Caroline.

She didn't mind in the least. He was fun, grounded, and ridiculously powerful for a mage even if his control and skill weren't very good yet. He was working on it.

"Meh, class. Classes are for people who aren't on a

'death-trudge' to an apartment," she answered, but she knew there was laughter in her voice. Even Spark could hear it because he laughed himself.

"I'm pretty sure death-trudge is a phrase you just made up," he said, amused. Caroline was about to respond when a voice interrupted her.

"Hey!" the urgent hiss came from the alley they were just passing. Caroline stopped dead. There was pain in that voice, and fear, and caution, and a bit of hope. It was also familiar. She turned to head into the shadows and Spark grabbed her shoulder.

"Hey, what are you doing?"

"I'm going to go help," she answered, shrugging him off.

"What if–" he started to say, then bit his words back.

"Like you're one to talk," she muttered and headed down the alley. "Besides, it's Lucas."

"Lucas?"

Caroline heard the frown in his voice more than saw it, but he followed her. There, half crumpled behind the dumpster behind the sandwich shop, huddled Lucas.

"I heard you coming. I've been hoping you wouldn't be too much longer," he said. "I was sort of hoping you'd let me clean up a bit in your apartment. I've had a bit of a rough couple of days."

"God. I'll say," she agreed. Lucas was ordinarily a pretty well-put-together sort of guy. She didn't want to assume that he ironed his jeans and polo shirts, but he sort of gave off the impression that he did. Today, though, he was rumpled and filthy, and one eye was bloodshot and a dark purple bruise spread over his cheek just below it.

"Are you bleeding? Should we call an ambulance? What happened?"

"No ambulance, I don't have time to lounge around in a hospital bed. I'm not bleeding anymore, no, and nothing's broken. I'm going to be sore as hell for a few days in the rib area, though. And you know, this eye is going to be a pain in my butt."

"Actually, I suspect it will be a pain in your eye," Spark said with a grimace. "I have all the luck with men behind dumpsters. Can you walk? Should we be on the lookout for whoever did this to you?"

"I can walk. I just need a shower, a meal, and some clean clothes. I can get two of those things at your place, I hope, C. And some time to catch my breath."

She pressed her lips together to prevent the irritated words that were building up from spilling out and nodded sharply. "I've got some sweats from work that should mostly fit you. Julia is on a business trip till next Thursday. She was mad she couldn't take me somewhere insane for spring break this year, so we'll have some peace and you can tell us what the hell happened."

"I really shouldn't–" he started.

"You'll tell us everything," she said. "Don't make me call Point."

Lucas grinned, though it was weak and he winced when the split in his lip stretched slightly. At least it didn't start bleeding again, and he flicked his tongue over it.

"Yes, ma'am," he agreed.

"Come on, I'll help you up, man." Spark leaned down and snaked a careful hand around Lucas under his right arm.

"At least you can mostly support yourself," he grunted as Lucas got onto his feet. "And you're about a third of the size of the last beat-up guy I helped out from behind a dumpster."

Spark had found Greg, roughed up and drugged and

hiding behind a dumpster near his old apartment almost a year earlier. It was how he had come to know them all, and turned out to be the beginning of the downfall of his crazy father.

Funny how everything seemed so damn connected, Caroline marveled as they ducked further down the alley to the small cross street behind. Lucas leaned on Spark but seemed to mostly be able to support himself as they made their way to Caroline's apartment. Once there, Spark dropped his satchel and helped Lucas into the bathroom while Caroline went looking for clean towels and something for Lucas to wear that wasn't covered in...whatever that all was. She suspected at least some of those smudges were blood.

Once she had his filthy clothes in the small washing machine in the nook behind the kitchen and a fresh pot of coffee brewing, she started pulling out eggs to make everyone something to eat. A nice, big omelet would feed them all and give her time to question her friend. The smell of the mushrooms sautéing in butter filled the apartment as she chewed her lip.

Lucas was in trouble. Caroline tried to sort through the scattered bits of information she had picked up.

"He's exhausted, but at least he's not passing out. I'm pretty sure there's no massive head injury to worry about," Spark said when he came back into the kitchen. "I left the sweats on the counter for him. That smells amazing."

"Thanks. Yeah. He's got some explaining to do," she answered. "Though, honestly, considering how I met him, I'm not shocked to find that someone finally caught up to him. Could you make some toast?

Spark's eyebrows rose even as he moved to follow her directions. "How did you meet?"

So Caroline finished the omelet and slid it onto some

plates while she told him about the awful frat party she went to her freshman year, looking for information, and how they had managed to crack open a human trafficking ring.

"You forgot the part where they tried to sell you to Darien as a snack." Lucas's voice was full of amusement. "Something smells fantastic out here."

"That was pretty funny. Now sit. Eat." She pointed at a chair and Lucas sat down, careful of what must have been painful ribs.

"Nothing's broken. I promise," he said when she cleared her throat. "And I did beat the guy in the end. He was just damned good at his job."

"And what was the guy's job?" Spark asked, setting the plates on the table. Caroline followed him with the coffee pot, mugs, and a small pitcher of milk. To think she had teased Julia about having serving trays.

After a few minutes of quiet eating, Lucas sighed. "He was a professional thug, and not a low-level one. An upper-tier thug, if you will. An apprentice henchman, maybe. He was damned good at what he did, that's what I know for sure." Lucas grimaced. "I wasn't even doing anything I shouldn't have been. I took a walk in a park to enjoy the weather, then I headed over to pick up a few things for my grandfather, not that he deserves to have me running his errands, but it's hard to break that sort of training, you know? My folks always drilled into me respect for my family, and the elders in it especially, and ugh. Maybe he should try showing me a little respect? Just because I refused to let him match-make me with some woman I've never met and have no interest in—"

"Lucas." Caroline tapped her finger next to his plate.

"Sorry. He's been being a serious pest lately." Lucas's grimace turned slightly long-suffering for a moment. "Anyhow, I was walking from the lake to the pharmacy and I wasn't even past the trees when this guy stepped out in front of me. I tried to politely get past him, and he grabbed my arm and dragged me off the path and out of easy sight, although if anyone walked past they could have heard us pretty easily."

"What did he want? I take it this wasn't a standard mugging," Spark said, refilling his cup.

"It took me a while to figure that out, actually. The guy never came out and said. He just kept asking 'Where is it?' and 'We know you took it' and ' Who hired you?' That sort of thing. I was a little busy defending myself to puzzle it out at the time. I managed to snatch up a branch that was lying on the ground, knocked him in the head, and got away while he was still woozy."

Lucas used his toast to scoop up the last of the eggs and cheese that was left and took a long gulp of his coffee before closing his eyes with a small smile. "Thank you for the meal, that was excellent."

Caroline blinked. "You're welcome. Still hungry?"

"I will let this settle first, then maybe we could have a snack later if you're still feeling generous."

"So, what did you figure out the guy wanted?" Spark leaned over the table, pushing his empty plate aside.

"Sorry." Lucas ducked his head. "I'm exhausted and distractible at this point, and the pain meds have kicked in so I'm sleepy too. Anyway, when I got away from the guy, I went by my house through the back way, just in case, and the place had been tossed. I mean, the whole place. Sofa cushions pulled apart, bookshelves emptied, drawers yanked out of the dresser. It was like a 'Goons Searching a House 101' practical exam. I just turned around and left. Didn't even touch anything. While I was making my way up here I figured out what the guy must have been looking for."

"Well?" Caroline demanded.

Lucas sighed and eyed her, then Spark for a long moment, then sighed again. "Well, you already know that I will stick my nose into about anything, private investigation license or not. I have the skills to track people down or find lost things."

"Yeah. We know, Lucas." Caroline narrowed her eyes at him. "That *was* you involved with that antiquities bust, wasn't it? And the grateful Egyptian government?"

Lucas had the good grace to look bashful. "So, you've figured me out, huh?"

Caroline just shot him a disdainful look.

"Okay, okay. I know. You're all super-smart secret agents. I get it," he said.

"Wait, I don't get it," Spark cut in. "I'm not any sort of agent, secret or not. What antiquities?"

Lucas sighed and sat back in the chair. "I've gotten a bit of a reputation for being able to find hard-to-track items. Missing people, family heirlooms that have disappeared after a death, proof of some kind of wrongdoing. I don't go out of my way to find jobs that are a little less than legal, but they have a way of finding me."

"What he means is that he's some sort of unholy lovechild of a white-hat hacker and a classic gentleman thief. He's practically his own anime character," Caroline said with a raised eyebrow.

"Hey, I could have let my grandfather marry me off and stick me in some dusty cube farm. Or gone the route a couple of the others like me have gone and put my services up for sale to whoever wants them no matter how unethical. I've spent a lot of time protecting banks and governments," Lucas grumbled. "I'm only one mage."

It was Caroline's turn to sigh. "I know, I know. And we're all glad you're on our side. But what happened today?"

Lucas grimaced, wincing when the split in his lip pulled again. "What happened is that I trusted the wrong lady, and now I think I'm in trouble."

5

"I'd say you're definitely in trouble, man," Spark pointed out. He stood up and collected the plates before rinsing them and stacking them all in the sink.

"Yeah, well," Lucas agreed.

Caroline didn't like the way his shoulders slouched at the statement. "Okay," she said. "How's this: we all refill our cups and head into the living room where it's a bit comfier, and you can start at the beginning. Okay?"

They agreed and once the table was cleared they moved. Lucas wasn't allowed to help.

Once Caroline had him settled on the sofa to her satisfaction, tucked in with a fresh cup of coffee and two pillows supporting him where he was curled up on the end, she pulled a blanket out of the closet and tossed it over the back in case he got cold, and got two pairs of raised eyebrows for that.

"What? I like to snuggle when all I'm beat up. Peaches isn't taking it nice and gentle with me in the training ring anymore. He's using, like, half-strength. It's *brutal*."

Spark snickered and Lucas just shook his head.

"Anyway," Caroline dragged the word out a bit longer than necessary. "I think Lucas has a story to tell us."

"Okay, so last year, just a bit before I met you, I took a job. It didn't seem like a big thing, which should have probably been my first clue." Lucas took a sip of his coffee and frowned at it.

"It was a friend of a friend sort of situation. Back when I was just starting out, I helped out a guy that belongs to my grandfather's club. It's this old-rich-men sort of thing, just with fewer entitled white guys, 'cause Grandfather is many things but entirely stupid isn't one of them. Anyhow, one of them heard that I was really good at tracking things down, and asked for my help when their brother's will went missing. It was a whole thing: the guy had made a new one every other week just about, but the one that was missing was made just a few days before he died, and he supposedly disinherited his wife. Anyway. I helped the guy out, found the will, and we all went away happy enough."

"Isn't it dangerous for people to know who you are? What you can do?" Spark asked from the overstuffed armchair that Julia liked best for movie nights.

"Yeah, well. For most stuff, I just explain that I am excellent at research and puzzle-solving, and I tell them that I outsource the rest," Lucas said. "Well, fast forward a few years, and I guess he had mentioned that I helped out finding this will, and next thing I was getting a phone call for a meeting at a restaurant near the club."

"You were summoned?" Spark's voice was laced with sympathetic understanding. No doubt he had the experience of receiving a summons from his father who felt that he was just that important.

Caroline was of the opinion that people who behaved that way were rarely as important as they thought.

Lucas chuckled. "I guess you could put it like that. It

was a call to my work phone. So, I called the number back which freaked the guy out a bit since he thought he had the information blocked, I guess, and explained that I don't do in-person meetings for everyone's safety. That's a straight-up lie, but anyone calling that number and *demanding* my presence isn't going to get it."

"Good call," Spark agreed.

"After a great deal of back and forth calling and several increasingly hostile messages left in the voicemail, the calls stopped entirely. Which made me very nervous." Lucas shook his head and stared at the coffee table for a moment. "I did some digging. It wasn't exactly complicated for me to trace one of the calls when I answered it, so I knew who had called. And after a bit of thinking, I figured out what they were probably after. But..."

"But?" Caroline prompted when he seemed to run out of steam.

"Okay." Lucas drew a deep breath. "I'm going to back up a little. A while ago—just a little before I met you like I said—I took this case where a woman got in touch with me. She had just inherited some stuff from her husband who had passed away, but the one thing she really wanted was the family heirloom that brought them together. It was explicitly left to her in the will, but it's a valuable antique and the guy's kids managed to make it disappear before the lawyers could get in and sort the whole mess out. So she hoped I could find it and return it to her."

"I take it that wasn't actually the whole story?" Caroline shifted on her end of the sofa, settling in for storytime.

Lucas sighed and seemed to deflate a bit. "I might be a bit of a sucker for a good romance story, and she spun a good tale. Still, I'm not an idiot, so I dug into it a little. She wasn't kidding that the thing was involved in her getting together with her husband, and it's not something that's *wildly* valuable. Not compared to the rest of the estate. So, I figured out where the kids stashed the thing. It was an antique dagger, medieval, and surprisingly plain, considering. Just a long slightly tarnished blade and a leather and bone grip."

He started to shrug, but stopped short and grimaced. "It was interesting from an arms history point of view, maybe, but otherwise pretty boring and the value was almost entirely in the historic connections it had, from what I could tell. It passed through the hands of a number of important people. But, and here's the thing, the husband had *loved* it. It was on his desk at all times, and he was known for touching and fiddling with it while he had meetings. Like a fidget toy for a kid."

"Okay, that's weird," Spark said. "That's evil-villain-level weird."

"You getting familiar megalomaniac vibes from it?" Caroline asked.

"A little," Spark admitted. His father was a real piece of work.

"Well, I wish I'd had you around back then," Lucas said. "Turns out the guy was actually a low-level-but-rising-fast criminal named Jeffery Calder. His kids were walking in the old man's footsteps, and it's possible that they helped him along, if you get my drift. I didn't really care too much about that, though if I could have found any incriminating evidence I'd have turned it over. The dagger wasn't the romantic momento I was told. I don't know what it really is, though. I just know that once I had it in my possession and called to report in to my client, a stranger answered and demanded I return the thing to the rightful heirs of my client's estate."

"Wait, your client's estate?" Caroline interrupted.

Lucas shot her a bland look and his voice was dry as

bone when he said, "She had been in an unfortunate car accident. The brakes on her vehicle failed unexpectedly and she drove right in front of an eighteen-wheel truck."

"Oh crap!" Spark hissed, and Caroline felt her eyes widen.

"This is straight out of some kind of criminal soap opera," she said.

"Yeah. Well, the ass who informed me of all this was smug as hell, so your suspicions are probably right," Lucas said with a sigh. He stretched a bit to put his empty mug on the coffee table. "God, everything aches," he groaned. Caroline patted his knee and he settled back into the cushions.

"At any rate, I dodged out of the whole situation pretty quick, ditched that phone, and erased all traces of the connection. At least I thought I had. The woman might have written things down physically. In a journal or a notebook or something. Who knows?"

They sat with the story for a long while, Lucas drifting off to sleep where he sat, his head leaning onto the back of the sofa. Caroline shook the blanket out and draped it over him.

"It's weird seeing him all rumpled in my emergency sweatpants and gym shirt. I mean, I'm glad he's not any taller or he'd look ridiculous," she said quietly.

Spark snorted. "You're not wrong. I wasn't expecting him to be quite so toned though. I guess I always thought that he did the stereotypical geek thing and never left his computer chair, but I'm not mad that shirt's a little snug."

Caroline threw a pillow at him. "Men are such horndogs."

Spark grinned, unrepentant. "What can I say? I'm not going to avoid the eye candy when it's paraded in front of me." He threw the pillow back. "And don't pretend you weren't looking, too, lady."

Caroline just smirked and stayed silent.

"What do you think of his story?" Spark asked softly.

Caroline grimaced. "Every word was truthful. He's gotten into something serious again."

"We should call Greg," Spark said.

"No," Lucas mumbled. He blinked a few times and rolled his head to look at Spark.

"Why not? You got jumped by a thug in the employ of some criminal dynasty. Greg would know who to talk to about keeping you safe," Spark argued.

"First, we don't know that this situation has anything to do with magic, which puts it outside the FPAA's authority. Second, did you forget the part where I stole something? I'd rather not get arrested, thanks."

"You're not going to get arrested. I assume nobody can connect you to the original job?" Spark argued.

Lucas frowned. "I thought that, too, until I got jumped and my house was ransacked."

Caroline wrinkled her nose. "Good point. Someone knows something."

"And once I've gotten some sleep I intend to find out who and what," Lucas said. He sat up a bit and rolled his shoulders. "And I try to swim laps every day when I'm not saving the world or getting chased by goons. I'm not just a geek-themed thief, you know." He started to grin at Spark but ended up yawning.

"Oh for the love of...Come on. There's a fold-out sofa in the office. I hear it's actually comfortable if Julia's cousin is to be believed." She stood and led him to it, opening the bed out and fluffing up a few pillows before tucking him in. "For now, you're safe and sound. We can decide what to do later after you've gotten some rest." She glared at him until he nodded.

"Okay. I don't sleep well on buses when I'm running for my very life, after all. Once I've had a nap, I'll come up with a plan."

"*We* will come up with a plan," she corrected him. "If you think I'm letting you run off into this mess on your own, you're not as smart as I thought."

"Aww, you do care," Lucas answered, but his words were slow. He was already falling asleep.

Caroline shook her head and huffed a small laugh before quietly closing the door and heading back to the living room.

"He all settled?" Spark asked. His coffee mug was full again, and another pot gurgled away in the kitchen.

"Out like a blown fuse. He must be hurting. Last time he went down that fast was after we found you and Greg, and that was after two days of no sleep and intense magic use." She flopped back down on the sofa and noticed that Spark had refilled her coffee as well.

"This isn't how I expected to start my spring break," she said.

Spark grinned. "You weren't going to the beach, either."

"I could have," Caroline huffed. She tucked her feet up under one of the pillows and propped her arms across her knees.

"So what should we do?" Spark glanced down the hallway.

"That's a good question. Right now, I guess, let him sleep for a while. Then..." She shrugged. "Help him sort it out, I guess. Point made sure I took this week really off, so I don't even have work."

"You were actually going to take a vacation?"

Caroline scrunched up her face. "I think he expected me to go home to visit my parents, but they keep asking if I'm going to move home after graduation and get a job near them somewhere. Like they don't know I'm planning to join the FPAA full-time."

Spark's eyebrows shot up. "Really? I honestly thought you were already full-time. You're always in the office when you're not in class."

"The office is more fun," she said. "I sort of intended to join full time from the beginning, but I need a degree to get hired. That's why I'm majoring in criminal justice. It's a degree that will be sort of handy when I graduate to full agent."

"That's pretty reasonable. I'm just taking general studies courses right now. I'm not sure what I want to do now that I'm not hiding from Aldebrand," Spark said, slumping back into his chair.

Caroline nodded. "I can't even imagine. Being tracked and kidnapped by your own father." She shuddered. "Maybe I *should* go home and see my folks for a bit, once we get Lucas squared away. At least they're not that kind of crazy."

Spark just nodded agreement and sipped at his coffee again.

6

Lucas woke up just as Caroline and Spark were contemplating dinner. He came stumbling into the living room, his black hair sticking up in the back, his hands in front of his face covering an enormous yawn.

"Good morning, Sleeping Beauty!" Spark said once Lucas had closed his mouth and scrubbed his fingers back over his scalp.

Lucas blinked at them slowly and nodded. "Is it morning? Or are you being funny? I'm still groggy enough that I can't tell."

Caroline laughed. "We were just talking about dinner. You were asleep for about four hours."

"Ah. I should probably skip coffee then," he said before heading into the kitchen. "I'll have water, thanks."

"There's more painkillers by the coffee pot, too, if you need them!" Caroline called after him. After Lucas was settled on the sofa and a bit more awake, they decided to just order a pizza and be done with the whole problem of dinner.

"Now that's taken care of, what's our plan?" Caroline

asked. "You never said where this all went down – or why you're here, besides you know I'm a soft touch for friends in need."

Lucas snorted. "You're not so much a soft touch as you are loyal and eager to leap before you look. That said, once I figured out what this was all connected to, I thought I'd aim in the general direction of where I hid the thing, and you happened to be on the way. Since I did need a safe place to crash for a bit, I thought it was convenient."

It was Spark's turn to snort. "Sure."

Lucas ignored him. "The place I left it is back in North Carolina, but it was safer for me to get out of state while I healed up, and I guessed you would help me out. I thought about renting a bus station locker or a safe deposit box or something, but I don't know. Something about the whole caper felt like it needed an old-school solution. So I snuck into a place nearby and hid it in plain sight." He snickered. "Little Jeff actually took over the house for his own base. He's basically sitting on the thing and has no idea."

"I still think we should call Greg," Spark said.

"And do what, tell him that we need help stealing back the thing I stole?" Lucas asked. He snorted a laugh and shook his head. "No thank you. They'd toss me in a cell with a rusty, old-fashioned padlock and throw away the key."

"We tell them that you've got a *crime family* after you and let them help you from there," Spark shot back. "Since you're dead set on running headlong into trouble, I'll go with you. At least one person in the group will have some common sense," Spark said. He glared at them each in turn and sounded just like a dad expecting trouble.

"Just don't melt the place on us," Caroline grinned.

"Don't piss me off, then." Spark grinned back. "Seriously, though, Mitch and I have been working a lot on control. I shouldn't be accidentally creating any volcanoes on the East Coast."

"I am so glad I'm just a small-time thief and hacker. This fieldwork stuff is kind of awful," Lucas groaned. "And I would love to call in the badass super-agents, but I have no proof of anything except my own guilt. I figure if we can retrieve the dagger and find out what's so damn important about it that the kids are willing to sic their dogs on me like that, then we'll have something for the guys to sink their teeth into. Figuratively speaking."

"Well, it might help if we knew who the players were," Caroline pointed out. Lucas was about to answer when the doorbell buzzed. Once they were all resettled and had tucked into their pizza, Caroline prompted him again. "So who wanted this dagger?"

Lucas wiped his fingers on the paper napkin on his knee and grimaced. "Well, when the woman approached me, as I said, she presented herself as a grieving widow that was robbed of a personal memento," he said. He scrunched up his face and sighed. "I looked into the will, just to verify that she wasn't lying about it since that's not incredibly uncommon, I've found. She was honest enough about that, but she left out a few things. If I'd run a full background like I usually do, I would have found out that the grieving widow in question was Daphne Calder, wife of the late and largely unlamented Jeffery Calder, who as it turns out was a minor but active crime lord in the southeastern coast. He had his fingers in all kinds of illegal activities from Florida all the way up to here. When he died, somewhat unexpectedly, his widow and his kids started jockeying for who would take the reins. Like a damn fool, I didn't even run a search engine search on any of them. If I had I could have saved myself a lot of trouble."

"I think I've heard of that guy," Caroline said. "Some of the analysts at work were saying that the kids must not be as good as their father at running his empire since there were rumblings and rumors about them making mistakes the old man never would have. Apparently, Jeffery Calder was known for being very shrewd. It was nearly impossible to get anything past him."

"Well, the widow struck me as cunning in her own way. I only have the one brief interaction with Jeff, the son—well, with his agents anyhow—so I can't really speak to him or his sister. If they did, indeed, get away with two murders, then they've got some criminal skills at least."

Spark picked up another slice. "You don't have to be an evil genius to run an underground empire. You just need to be charismatic, a little clever, and rich."

"True enough," Lucas agreed. "At any rate, I checked out the will, saw that he had, indeed, left the damned thing to his wife, and off I went. The kids weren't even bothering to hide it, either. It was just sitting right there in the office they were using. Well, that he was using. The daughter doesn't want to actually run anything, it seems. She just thought her brother would get her the better end of the deal. I guess Mom wasn't very maternal."

"So you just strolled into Jeff's office, took this fancy dagger, and walked out? Then hid it somewhere? Why?" Caroline asked.

"Well, like I mentioned. At that point I was getting the feeling that something was a bit hinky," Lucas answered. "I wanted to be sure I was going to be safe if things hit the fan. And look how well that worked out for me."

"Why now, I wonder?" Caroline asked. "Why let it lie for over a year?"

"That I can't tell you. I've done as much digging into the players as I can, as far as I know them while on the run and trying not to get caught. Well, the kids I guess since the other two are dead. Maybe there's some sort of plan they need it for or they need the thing as proof of leadership?"

"Well, how're you feeling now? We should have asked when you came out here." Spark frowned at himself.

"Much better. It's amazing what a little sleep and the feeling that you're not about to get murdered can do to heal a body." Lucas reached up to prod at the bruise under his eye and winced. "Still a bit banged up, but better."

"Don't I know it? Constant alertness can be exhausting," Spark agreed.

"Well, maybe you can spend a little time looking into this Jeff and his sister, and maybe we can find out what changed. I can call Shakes and see if he has any information about the situation down there, beyond the family," Caroline said. "If I tell him that the power shift came up in conversation in a class and I got curious, he shouldn't be too nosy about it."

"If Darien or Point find out you're off having unsanctioned adventures, they're going to be pissed off," Spark pointed out. "You're planning trouble."

"You shouldn't get yourself in trouble for me, C," Lucas said. "I can do this on my own, I just needed a place to rest and reorient myself."

Caroline pinned Lucas with a stare so hard he flinched back a bit. "I am not sending you out, alone, to deal with some psycho crime lord who thinks stealing from each other and murdering his parents is perfectly fine."

Spark pressed his lips together for a moment before sighing and nodding. "I don't think that letting either of you out unsupervised is a good idea."

"Hey!" Caroline protested at the same time as Lucas said "I've done just fine till now, thank you!"

"Oh, yes. Just fine," Spark agreed solemnly, his gaze

pointedly sweeping over the purple bruise on Lucas's cheek.

"Oh, please. A couple of sucker punches are nothing," Lucas scoffed.

"I saw your ribs when I brought you the sweats," Spark said.

Lucas just winced and didn't answer.

"And as for you, Miss I-get-kidnapped-every-other-day, don't even get me started on some of the stories I've heard about you," Spark grumbled.

"Hey, I'm just an intern! How am I supposed to know what to do all the time?" Caroline protested. It sounded weak as hell to her and by the raised eyebrows on both men's faces, they weren't buying it either. "And that first time I was just skipping class in a place that should have been perfectly safe. That was not my fault at all."

"I'm not even going to touch that one," Spark muttered, then he cleared his throat. "My point is that you're not so good at looking before you leap and that neither of you seems to be terribly concerned about personal safety. Together you'll be working so hard to keep the other one safe at your own expense that you'll both run face-first into disaster."

Caroline glared at Spark and Lucas shifted in his seat. Spark just raised a smug eyebrow at her, daring her to argue with him.

"Nobody asked you," she huffed instead, and started cleaning up the remains of the pizza.

"So." Lucas coughed, then winced. "I guess we have a rudimentary plan then? We look into these people and what may have changed recently and go from there?"

"Sure. You can use my laptop if your tablet isn't enough for your research," Caroline said, waving her hand at her backpack.

"My tablet is pretty much saturated with my magic at this point. I almost don't even have to type on it to get it working." Lucas grinned. "It's almost like a cyberpunk implant now. When it finally dies I am going to hold a Viking funeral or something."

Caroline laughed and even Spark grinned.

"I'm pretty sure that burning electronics is unhealthy," Spark said.

"It's a long time from now, so we can figure something out, I'm sure," Lucas said with a cheeky grin.

"I bet Mitch will want it for study and preservation," Caroline called from the kitchen. "He's going to want to put it in a museum or something after he tests all the magical things."

Lucas snorted and Spark laughed out loud.

"It's true. He's going to want to dissect the thing and make you fill out a twenty-page questionnaire about it," Spark said.

Lucas sighed and slumped in his chair. "The worst part is that you're absolutely right. That guy's a machine when it comes to intellectual puzzles."

"And right here, in this room, are three of his very favorite puzzles." Caroline laughed. and flopped back onto the sofa. "You and your new evolution in magic, me with my empathy-adjacent abilities that we can't figure out, and Spark there with his rare combination of earth and fire magics."

"Oh lord, it's so true," Spark groaned. "I appreciate the hell out of his help. He worked with me almost every day for months after you guys saved me, just so I could learn what I can do and how not to do it accidentally. But good lord, if he asks me one more time to call fire in increasing one-millimeter size increments or shake a tray of dirt—but slower this time—I might start drinking."

Lucas grumbled his agreement. "Oh god. One more 'Now search for the closest pizza shop but don't type anything and do it very slowly, I'm watching the magic flow' or whatever, I'm going to lose it."

Caroline giggled. Mitch was a great friend, and happy to explain anything he knew, but he did get a bit hyper-focused and sometimes he forgot that the people he was working with were, well, people.

"Okay. Enough whining," Lucas said. He nodded firmly once and stood. "Okay. Mitch isn't here to watch and my tablet is nowhere close to electronic death, so I'm going to settle back onto the sofabed and dig into Jeff and his sister and anyone else that might be relevant. I'll let you guys know what's up in the morning. I think I'm probably going to fall asleep while working."

As if to punctuate his prediction, Lucas yawned so wide that Caroline thought she heard his jaw crack.

"Don't push yourself too hard, you still need to heal," she warned him. "I'll text Shakes and see if he's heard any chatter about anything that may be relevant. I'll tell him we were talking about the balance of power between crime families and stuff in class, and I got curious to see if there've been any recent shifts."

"Sounds good. You coming back tomorrow, Spark?" Lucas turned to the slim man in the overstuffed chair.

"Nope," he said. "I'm not leaving you two trouble-makers here on your own. I'll take the sofa."

Caroline grinned. She didn't like a quiet apartment anyway.

7

Morning came and Caroline woke to a gray drizzle of rain outside her window and the smell of coffee and bacon inside the apartment. She was not entirely awake when she reached the kitchen, which is probably why the sight of Spark grinning like a loon at Lucas's half-asleep face across the breakfast bar brought her up short.

"Morning, Sunshine." Spark turned his grin to her. "I've got you covered, grab a seat."

"Don't mind me, I was just enjoying having a kitchen full of cute boys," she replied.

"You think I'm cute?" Lucas perked up.

Spark snorted and shared an eyeroll with Caroline as he slid her a mug of coffee. Even with the bruise covering a quarter of his face, the man was striking and he damn well knew it.

"I'm making pancakes. You two wake up a bit, hmm?" Spark chuckled and turned back to the counter where he had ingredients lined up neatly.

"You're a morning person *and* you cook, too?" Caroline asked once she swallowed down half her coffee.

Spark shrugged. "When I got away from Aldebrand the first time I set about doing as many things as I could think of that he would hate. I got a service job, got a tiny, shitty apartment with two roommates, learned to cook. By the time Greg upended my life I'd been living on my own for more than long enough to have perfected a few favorite recipes."

"I should take photos of you in that jeans-and-apron combo making breakfast and looking so inexcusably cheerful for first thing in the morning and send it to him. Make him explain why he inflicted you upon us. Psychological torture is still frowned upon, even in the paranormal community." Caroline sighed, pretending to be disappointed.

"Yeah, yeah, Spark's very domestic. Back up, though," Lucas said, nudging her elbow. "You think I'm cute?"

Caroline and Spark both laughed and by the time the pancakes were eaten and the kitchen cleaned up, the subject had come back around to Lucas's little problem.

"So I got a quick overview from Shakes," Caroline said. "Apparently young Jeff isn't doing as amazing a job as dear old dad did, and a lot of people down there are grumbling. A cousin and at least one of the lieutenants in his organization have been making small plays to take over. It's unknown if Jeff is completely aware of it, though."

"That confirms what I heard as well. Just quiet rumblings and whispers right now, but that sort of thing spirals quickly," Lucas said.

"If he does know, this kid is one of two things: arrogantly confident in his position and thinks he's untouchable, or desperate and panicking," Spark said. "Aldebrand would get livid when someone questioned him even slightly, but he also didn't think he could get held accountable for anything."

Lucas nodded. "Not sure what that has to do with my job from last year, though."

"Well, if that dagger is a symbol of office, so to speak, then it could add strength to his claim," Spark said with a speculative stare out the window at the rain. "Or it could have some sort of important enchantment on it, like... I don't know. To kill someone with a tiny cut or something. Doesn't make much sense in a room full of guys armed with guns, but maybe."

"Or it could be the key to something that would strengthen his claim. Like a way to open a secret room or something," Caroline added. "Or maybe–"

A ringtone she didn't recognize cut her off and made Lucas frown. He reached into the pocket of his borrowed sweatpants and pulled a cheap phone from his pocket.

Signaling them both to stay quiet he answered the call.

"Hello? I can get a message to them, yes, what is this regarding? I see. I see." His eyebrows drew together as his frown deepened. "Are you in danger right now? Where are you? Okay, here's what you're going to do. Leave your car and your phone at your hotel and get a taxi somewhere public. Then take a different taxi to the address I will give you. Do you have a pen and paper?" Lucas's frown deepened as he listened for a long moment before he gave the caller the address of a café close to campus.

"I can understand that, ma'am, but if you're afraid that your contact is dirty then... That's right. And once you're safe you can go to the FPAA with your information. I have friends who can put you in touch with agents that are unquestionably clean. Very well. I'll arrange for someone to meet you there."

He hung up with his frown still firmly in place. "It seems that I'm not the only one being targeted. That was Ms. Lynn Graves, another cousin. Apparently, she was trying to go to the FBI with information on the 'family business' and felt like she was being followed for a bit before the planned meeting. When she got there yesterday, she saw young Jeff's right-hand man sitting where the agent told her he'd be, so she turned around and ran."

"And called you?" Spark's voice carried a healthy dose of skepticism.

Lucas shrugged. "She said she was close to her aunt and was with her when I was first hired, which is why she knew about me. Thought I would know a way for her to get away."

Caroline frowned. Something about the whole situation felt odd, but she couldn't put her finger on it. "You don't think the timing is a bit suspect?" Spark frowned.

"I do," Lucas answered. "But it makes sense, doesn't it? If Jeff Calder knows who I am well enough to have me roughed up and my house tossed, then he also knows I'm connected to the FPAA. All you government types overlap and feud and share information or hide it and we mere mortals never know which of you is working with who. So, maybe he wanted to make sure neither agency got the information."

"But we don't even have any information," Caroline pointed out. It still didn't feel quite right to her, but Lucas did have a point.

"But we do. Well, I do, anyhow. I know where the dagger is. What I don't know is why anyone wants the damn thing."

Spark sighed, started to speak, then waved his thought away.

"What?" Lucas asked.

"I still think we should call Greg. Or Darien." Spark shrugged. "Especially if an FBI agent has gone missing."

"Well, we don't know that there even was an agent. We

just know what Ms. Graves told Lucas," Caroline pointed out.

"And we have a meeting with her across town," Spark said.

"Which we really ought to get ready to head to. If you don't want to come I understand," Lucas said. He stood and stretched and his borrowed T-shirt lifted with the movement. "I just needed a safe place to crash for a while. Somewhere I could get some real rest instead of being half awake and on alert the whole time."

"I'm coming. You're not getting out of this all that easy, who knows what havoc you'll create," Caroline said. She stood as well. "Your clothes are in the dryer. I'm going to go get dressed. Spark?"

"Yeah," he sighed. "I'm coming. You two seem hellbent on having this little adventure. The least I can do is make sure there's a grown-up along."

At the coffee shop, which Spark wasn't impressed with, they found Lynn Graves seated at a table near the back. Lucas went over to her on his own, to avoid scaring the woman away, with Caroline and Spark picking a different table nearby, so they could watch without making the woman nervous.

"Do you buy her story?" Spark asked quietly once he was seated. There was enough chatter in the place, on top of the bland pop music to cover their conversation.

"Not even with a fake dollar," Caroline answered. "The timing is all sorts of convenient, and how did she track down Lucas? I know that he has a special number for 'work' stuff." She gave the word some heavily sarcastic airquotes. "And how did *anyone* connect him to the theft, if his client didn't tell them? I assume she didn't tell anyone before she died. And here's a question: does anyone know that Lucas and the thief are the same person or do they just think he's the thief's handler?"

Spark grimaced and picked a chocolate chip out of the scone on his plate.

"I wish we could hear what they were saying," he grumbled. "I don't like this cloak-and-dagger stuff. It feels like there's too much that could go wrong."

"Yeah. A nice, straightforward arrest would be lovely about now, huh?" Caroline agreed. "But even the FPAA has undercover operations. The first time I met Lucas, D went undercover. He was undercover when I was grabbed off campus, and thank goodness for that."

"It was a good thing you got grabbed?" Spark's tone told her just how unlikely he thought that was.

Caroline snorted. "No, I meant it was a good thing he was undercover. He was in exactly the place he needed to be to 'buy' me back. And when the kidnapping jerks were feeling extra paranoid and demanded that D taste his new snack right there it was fine, because he knows damn well I'll let him feed from me if he needs it."

She shrugged when Spark almost choked on his latte. "Not like it was the first time, either."

His eyes popped wide open. "Darien has fed from you? Directly?"

"Darien fed from me within about four hours of meeting me. I'll tell you the whole story sometime, but basically, we were both in a hell of a lot of trouble and he needed to heal enough that we could escape." She grinned suddenly. "Why do you think he calls me Sunshine all the time?"

"I thought it was because you're *such* a morning person and he's really good at sarcasm." Spark grinned.

"Nah." She snickered. "He says that's what my blood tastes like."

"Jesus," Spark muttered and took a long draw from his coffee. "Remind me to stop calling you that, too."

"I thought vampires got addicted to their, uh. Their donors," he asked. He stumbled over a few of the words, and when Caroline glanced at him he was turning pink. It was kind of adorable. "And isn't it illegal?"

"Well, sort of? I mean, no. It's not illegal, but it's frowned on pretty heavily in vampire culture, I guess. It's complicated and I don't really understand it all, even though I've lived through it several times now, but a direct bite will form a bloodbond, which has a few effects. The one that probably spawned that particular myth is that the vampire will become pretty protective of their, um, food source. I guess it's not super easy to find willing volunteers or something."

"Huh."

She glanced over at where Lucas was sitting with Lynn. "She's crying now, but not sobbing. Looks more like frustration and grief. Maybe she's talking about her aunt?"

"I still think this is way too convenient and we should get Greg here," Spark muttered.

Caroline grimaced. Spark was probably right if she was going to be honest with herself. Sitting here trying to figure out what's happening and dodging a mid-sized criminal organization without her team felt very odd, and not in a good way. Lucas knew what he was doing, though, and she had to trust that. This wasn't his first rodeo any more than it would be Greg's, or Darien's.

"I can't argue with you, honestly, but this is Lucas's show. If he doesn't feel like we can bring the guys in then…" She shrugged. "Besides, it sounds like a pretty simple in-and-out sort of thing to grab this dagger and then..."

"Exactly. And then what?" Spark leaned over the table. "Lucas can't just go off on his own all the time. He's going to get caught or killed. And you're almost as bad, C. Even if you're not on some official case, they're still your team."

"I know. It's just..." She wasn't even sure she understood it herself, truth be told. She scrunched up her nose and glared at her cappuccino. "I just don't think we need them for this part, I guess. Lucas is damn good at sneaking in and out of places. We'll get this dagger thing then call the guys. Mitch can check on whatever enchantment it has, and the rest of us can dig into the family. I just don't know if there's a real case for us here or if it's just a power struggle that's better left alone to leave fewer players on the board."

"Well, you'd better figure it out," Spark said glancing up. "Lucas is waving us over to chat with his new buddy."

8

Caroline slid into the booth next to Lucas and sent the startled woman a reassuring smile. Reluctance flashed through Spark's eyes, but he gently took the seat beside Lynn.

"This is Sunshine and Vulcan. They occasionally work with Robin as well, and considering what your cousin did to me, I asked for their help," Lucas said.

Caroline heard the warning to keep identities and information secret carry through his voice as clearly as if he had said the words. She glanced at Spark and saw amusement and understanding in his eyes.

"At this point—I hope you'll forgive—but trust comes at a premium," Lucas finished.

"No, that's sensible," she agreed. She turned to Caroline and tried to smile, then nodded to Spark. "It's good to meet you both."

Caroline looked over the woman. She wore a T-shirt and a light jacket, perhaps trying to blend in a bit, but if that was the case, Lynn wasn't doing a very good job. Everything about her screamed pampered and wealthy.

She looked tired, though. Her bright blond hair was swept into a perfect updo and her makeup was flawless, but there was a dullness in her gaze and not even the expensive foundation she wore completely covered up the smudgy circles under her eyes.

"So, what can you tell us about this situation?" Caroline asked.

Lynn sighed and ran her fingers over the handle of her cappuccino cup.

"My uncle was…" She pinched her lips together for a moment. "He was not a nice man. He was a confusing man, and good to his family, to those he cared about, but ruthless with everyone else. Growing up I knew him to be a doting uncle. It wasn't until I was older that I understood…" She dropped her gaze to her fingers.

"Well, that's still an improvement over the last major criminal I dealt with," Spark grumbled. "Nice to know that at least some crime bosses are decent to kids."

Lynn's eyebrows shot up and she looked at him with a small frown. "Yes, well. My aunt was always taking me and my cousin Kelsie shopping and to tea and so on. Kelsie never much cared for anything but the shopping, but I loved it. Hanging out with them. Aunt Daphne and I grew very close, which was good since my own mom died when I was young. Cancer."

They all grimaced. It was a subject that almost everyone could find common ground on.

"I'm glad you had a good childhood," Lucas said softly.

"Thank you. When I was old enough to understand where the money came from, I tried to distance myself a bit. My father was not involved in any of it, as far as I can tell, though he never said a word against it all. He simply ran his restaurants and ignored what his brother was doing." She shrugged. "I studied hard and went to college, all of that stuff, but I still loved my aunt and uncle. Even knowing what he did couldn't stop that. I think they understood my feelings on it and made sure not to talk about any of their, er, business when I was around."

Caroline strained her ears, tried to stretch out with whatever power she had, and tried to keep the frown off her own face. Lynn's words were ringing true to Caroline's ears, but…it was tinny and thin, like the truth was being shouted down a long, empty tunnel. It wasn't like anything she had ever encountered before and it left her feeling a bit greasy and uncomfortable.

"So what does this have to do with the current situation?" Spark asked. "I'm sorry for your loss, and for the fact that they put you in such an awkward position, but…" Spark's eyes flicked up to the bruise on Lucas's face. "How do we keep everyone safe, now?"

Lynn frowned but nodded. "There have been rumors lately. About another criminal wanting to move into Uncle Jeffery's territory. My cousin JJ—er, Jeffery Calder Junior. The family calls him JJ. Anyway, he's in charge of it all now. I think… I think that Aunt Daphne was supposed to take over after Uncle Jeffery died, but then she was in that accident."

Lynn's eyes grew glassy and Caroline had the sense that the grief was genuine. Spark rubbed a reassuring hand over Lynn's shoulder. Lynn turned and sent him a small smile.

"I'm convinced that JJ had something to do with that, but I have no proof," she said after a moment. "But he's getting worried now. He hasn't really gotten as firm a grip on the organization as he would like, I think, and the possible threat to his leadership is irritating him."

Lucas nodded. "That makes sense. It often takes years for a new leader to cement the necessary loyalty. A threat to his leadership so soon after he took it up would make him nervous. It *should* make him nervous."

"But what does that have to do with..." Caroline glanced over at Lucas.

"Mister, er..." Lynn's lips twitched at the corners and genuine mirth shone in her eyes. "Mr. Smart here is the only known contact for the man who was hired to steal my uncle's knife. That knife was the symbol of Uncle Jeffery's authority. The story I was told is that he took it from the man who was trying to build an empire where Uncle Jeffery wanted to settle. Well. Took it *out* of him. That's what they meant. It was always on his desk when he was doing business, and he always took it to meetings when he went somewhere else to have them. He even had a special sheath made to carry it in, all leather and fancy scrollwork and a special enchantment to make it harder to notice until he took it out to casually play with it while he negotiated."

"A threat and a reminder of what he can do," Spark murmured.

Lynn grimaced and nodded. "Exactly. After so long, it was understood that whoever he passed that knife to was his official heir and the next leader of his organization. When it disappeared so soon after he died, the legend sort of grew."

Lucas chuckled. "Like the underworld's version of Excalibur. Whosoever shows up with this dagger is the rightful king of the criminals. And another reason your cousin's grip on power is so tenuous."

Lynn chuckled lightly. "Something like that, I suppose."

The thready nature of the truth in Lynn's words was setting Caroline's teeth on edge. She wanted more than anything to call the woman out on her lies–but they *weren't* lies–and it was making Caroline a little nuts. "You said he had a sheath enchanted for it. Is it possible it's simply sitting in that sheath and people are walking right past the thing?"

Lynn shook her head. "It only works when the dagger is being worn. Like on a belt. It needs to be worn for the enchantment to be activated. And it would still *be* there. Getting a weapon past casual inspection when it is worn and deliberately looking for it on a desk or a shelf are two different things."

"So, what is it that you came to us for?" Spark asked after they had all sat with the story for a moment. "To ask Robin where the knife ended up?"

"I'm not sure." Lynn grimaced. "Jeff has been casting around, trying to find who could be turning against him. He accused me of taking the knife and hiding it because I didn't like the family business. I told him that *my* family business was a chain of restaurants and bars, but he just stormed out of the room. I thought…" She sighed and shrugged and went back to staring at her mug.

"I don't know. I suppose I thought that if that knife was found then maybe he would stop behaving so strangely. I don't care what happens to it. I just don't want to get murdered in my own bed. Or hit by a truck while I'm driving home from lunch." Her lips thinned into a flat line and she looked up at Lucas, then at Caroline and Spark. "If you can get a message to Robin. Ask him where the thing went, or maybe convince whoever has it to show it in public... something?"

Caroline's brain itched. Something about this woman was setting off all sorts of red flags, but no matter how hard she listened, she only heard what Lynn's words portrayed: anxiety, fear, and a touch of desperation. Lucas's gaze flicked to check in and she knew what he was looking for, so she answered his silent question, but frowned as she nodded.

"Well, Lynn." Lucas said. He smiled warmly and reached to pat Lynn's wrist. "We'll see what we can do. I'll get in touch with Robin and see what he has to say and if he has any ideas. Is there a good way to get in touch with you?"

Lynn nodded. "I called you from my cell phone." She made a face and shrugged. "I figured that with my criminal cousin killing off family members, using my regular phone to get in touch with a thief was the least of my worries."

Lucas chuckled. "Now, do you have a safe place to be for a while?" he asked.

"I have no idea, frankly. I didn't think Jeff was paying much attention to me, but apparently I was wrong. I didn't expect Pietro. I don't know how he knew I was coming up here."

"How did you make the arrangement to meet the agents?" Caroline asked.

"I make all my calls from my office. Well, almost all of them," she answered. "I hope he's okay. Agent James Carter. He wasn't there when I got to the hotel, and then I saw Pietro and just left. I didn't even check in."

Lucas tapped another note into his phone, moving much slower than Caroline was used to seeing when he typed. "We'll see if we hear anything about him, too. Not that I have many contacts in law enforcement." He winked at Lynn and she smiled back briefly before dropping her gaze back to the now empty cup.

"I'd guess your office is bugged," he said. "And probably your home as well. It might be worthwhile for you to get a new phone, also, to make sure that he hasn't put any tracking software on that one. If your cousin is really as paranoid as you have implied, I wouldn't put it past him."

"Or my brother." Her lips thinned again. "He and JJ

have always been tight. But that's another problem for another day."

"Family drama is the most exciting drama, isn't it?" Spark sighed.

Lynn's small smile reappeared and she glanced over at him. "You have some family drama, too, Vulcan?"

Spark shrugged. "I did. It's been cleared up now, but it got rather hot there for a bit."

Caroline bit the inside of her cheek to keep from laughing.

"How did yours resolve?" Lynn asked.

"FPAA raid." Spark grinned. "Lots of arrests."

Lynn blinked, not expecting that answer. "Oh."

"So," Lucas cut in. He dug into his bag for a moment before pulling an old phone out and handing it to Lynn. "Take this phone. It's clean and the only number on it is one you can use to get in touch with me. Write any important numbers you have down on a piece of paper, then ditch your old phone somewhere far from where you're staying." He waited until she nodded before continuing.

"What I suggest you do is find a safe place to stay for the next few days. We'll be in touch after we talk to Robin."

"I can't…" Lynn glanced around the café at the bright, hipster decor and the cheerful mix of college students and businesspeople scattered around. "I can't stay with you?" Her tone turned pleading.

"I don't think that's a very good idea," Caroline shook her head. "If you're being followed or tracked, we don't want to draw attention to Robin and your cousin seems to be paranoid but not stupid."

Also, much more time in this woman's presence and Caroline wasn't sure what she would do. Lynn Graves was giving her a headache.

Lynn turned wide eyes to Lucas, who tipped his head in thought.

"I think, for now at least, it wouldn't be wise," he said. "We need the freedom to move, and I hope you don't take offense, but we can't do that with a civilian around, for lack of a better word."

"I suppose I can understand that," Lynn answered slowly. She started to say something else, but then bit her lip and glanced up at Lucas. "And I suppose it gives me plausible deniability. I can say that I just met up with some friends and complained about my troubles."

Lucas leaned forward slightly, a charming grin on his face. "That's very true."

After a few more minutes of watching Lynn flirt with Lucas, and to a lesser degree with Spark who visibly found her efforts amusing, Lynn Graves headed out of the café to her new hotel.

"Well?" Lucas turned to Caroline.

She knew what he was asking.

"Nothing she said was a lie," she answered but she shook her head and scowled. "But I still don't believe her. There's something very off about that woman. She wasn't lying exactly, but I'm not convinced she was telling the truth either."

"Come on, C. You can't fake the truth," Lucas said with a smile. "We can sort the rest out later."

9

Back at Caroline's apartment, the three of them resumed their seats in the living room. Caroline turned on the TV and started flipping through the channels without paying them a great deal of attention. Lucas dug his tablet out of his bag and his fingers started flying over the screen.

"Her office phone is, indeed, bugged. And there's at least two viruses on her office computer watching what she does. And there's an app on her cell phone, though that will be easy enough to deal with if she took my advice on ditching her phone."

Caroline sighed, and stretched her legs out to prop her feet on the coffee table.

"You didn't like her much, did you, C?" Spark said with a grin.

Lucas's head snapped up. "You didn't?"

Caroline scrunched up her face. "There was something about her that really just made my teeth itch, as my grandmother would have said."

Lucas frowned and tipped his head. His dark hair slid

into his eyes and Caroline wondered if he left it long enough to do that on purpose.

"I thought you said she wasn't lying? Did you pick up anything else? Any stray information?" he asked. "I know you do sometimes."

She shook her head slowly. "Nothing. And yeah, my weird, impossible-to-train, won't-behave-on-command talent said that she wasn't lying, but…"

Spark grinned. "No, no, no. That's not what I meant. You didn't like her flirting."

"Flirting?" Lucas blinked. He turned a confused look to Spark.

Spark snorted. "Don't even start, you were flirting back."

Lucas didn't respond and Caroline tried not to be annoyed with all of them.

"Whatever," Caroline said. "I don't trust her."

Lucas turned to gaze at her for a few long moments before he turned back to his tablet.

"So, what are we going to do?" Caroline asked. She finally settled on an old sitcom rerun that nobody would pay much attention to and put the remote down.

"I'm going to go retrieve the dagger. Maybe once we have it in hand we can see what's so damn special about it that everyone's so interested in," Lucas said, eyes on his tablet. "I don't trust that it's just some sort of underworld Excalibur. Jeff is frothing at the mouth to find it. There's whispers that a cousin is searching for it—it was the cousin's goon that caught up with me apparently, but Jeff's goons that searched my house. It seems that there's been a fair amount of chatter surrounding the thing."

"How did they find you, anyway?" Spark asked. "That's my biggest concern, to be honest."

Lucas grimaced. "I wasn't especially careful in the

beginning of my career. Remember when I said that my grandfather's friend had recommended me to the grieving Widow Calder? I'd guess that's how they tracked me down. Mrs. Calder knew my name, more than likely, so if she had it written down anywhere it would be pretty easy to find me. I'm not the world's only hacker, you know."

"Just one of the very few that uses magic to do it, instead of code," Spark said with a grin. Lucas just shrugged.

"If they had your real name, they probably didn't even need to hack anything. Just do an internet search," Caroline pointed out. "And back up for a second. You're going to retrieve the dagger? You seem to be under the impression we're going to let you go anywhere on your own."

Lucas did look up from his tablet at that. "Huh?"

Caroline tried not to smile at the confusion in that one syllable. "You're sort of cute when you lose the thread."

"I haven't lost anything. What do you mean you're not letting me go anywhere?" he asked.

Spark snorted and stood up. "You two work this out and let me know, I had too much coffee to sit through this argument. I'll be back in a minute."

Caroline watched Spark's retreating back for a moment before turning back to Lucas.

"Did you honestly think you could stumble in here, hide out for a day with bruises all over, then just head off on your own again?" Caroline demanded. She sat up and glared at Lucas. "I've seen some of the stunts you pull, forget it."

Lucas blinked at her. "You... You want to come with me? But what about school? Work?" He gestured vaguely at the window and Caroline had no idea what he thought he was indicating. "You know, everything."

"I had my last class before spring break yesterday. I

have plenty of time to go with you to wherever and watch your back while you break into some ridiculous place to snatch this thing. Then we are going to let this Jeff guy know that you are about to melt the damn thing down if his goons don't lay off."

Lucas blinked at her and she wondered if maybe she was being too pushy. One glance at the purple splotch down his face and she pushed that thought away.

"Caroline, I don't think that would work," Lucas sighed. "I think I'm going to have to get this dagger and find out why they want it so badly, yes, but then I'm going to be doing a lot more digging, and probably have to disappear for a while." He groaned and scrubbed his hand down his face. "This is going to make a mess of my whole life. Grandfather is going to have an aneurysm when I don't show up to his next charity event."

The change of subject came out of left field. "Charity event?"

"Yeah," Lucas groaned again. "Grandfather makes me go to these events every couple of months in the expectation that I'll let him set me up with a woman to marry. He wants me to start producing heirs for his own personal dynasty or something. He's nowhere near as bad as Spark's gene donor was, but he's damn pushy about it."

Caroline blinked at the frustration and grudging sense of duty Lucas's words carried. He laughed suddenly.

"You know, he'd consider Lynn Graves acceptable." Lucas snickered. "She's wealthy and attractive. We can just pretend that she doesn't come from a crime family. I'm not sure Grandfather would care all that much, anyway."

A sour feeling settled in Caroline's stomach and she forced herself to stay on topic. "Okay, none of this had anything to do with anything," she said. Hopefully she didn't sound as annoyed as she felt for some reason. "Disappearing isn't going to fix anything."

"She's right," Spark agreed. He flopped back into his chair and peered at Lucas. "I take it your grand plan is to just go away until the dust settles? Trust me. The dust does not settle. It just waits."

"I don't think that these guys are thinking as long-term as your—as Aldebrand was." Lucas sucked in a deep breath and started to scrub his hands over his face before it hit his bruise. He grunted and dropped his hands. "Guys, just let me take the attention off you, please?"

"Nope." "Get over yourself." Spark and Caroline spoke at once, then exchanged a look.

"Let's go over it. Maybe I can convince you to take it to the guys," Spark said. He leaned forward, elbows on knees, and started ticking off points on his fingers. "You have a not-super-legal business of retrieving things from people who shouldn't have them." Next finger. "On probably more than one case, you didn't do enough research and as a result you stole something dangerous." Middle finger. "The woman that hired you wasn't terribly discreet and upon her death, the person you removed the item from wants it back and knows who you are." Pointer finger. "You have been tracked down, beaten up, and nearly dragged back to Junior."

Lucas took up the count now. "We know that Calder Senior used the dagger as a badge of office of sorts, and honestly, probably also a threat. The thing is a weapon, after all. We know that he meant to leave it – and his burgeoning empire – to his widow, and his son took over through manipulation and maybe murder. We know we can't prove any of this except the 'Lucas is a semi-professional thief' part which will, I'd like to remind you, get Lucas arrested."

Caroline sighed now. "We also know that Jeff Junior is watching his cousin and wants to keep this all away from law enforcement. The question I have is does he know about Lucas's connection to me and the FPAA office here in Stonehaven, or is Lynn's meeting near here a coincidence. Lucas, did she sound surprised to be meeting you here and not back in Marsden or wherever she lives?"

Lucas tipped his head to rest on the back of the sofa and glared at the ceiling while he thought. "I... I think she was just relieved to have an ally. I don't remember her sounding especially surprised, but she didn't sound like she was getting confirmation, either."

"Wish I'd been able to talk to her. I could have picked that up, probably," Caroline grumbled.

"Okay, so, our guess is that Jeff Calder knows that you're here, and he probably knows who you're hanging out with. Especially if he's been following Lynn. Meeting with her in person wasn't the brightest move, Lucas," Spark said.

"She just sounded so freaked out. It's much easier to reassure someone in person than it is over the phone," Lucas protested.

"True, and you're the sort of man who hates to hear someone frightened or miserable," Spark agreed. "Lynn Graves appeared to be both. And she's grieving for her aunt, as well as carrying suspicions that the woman was murdered."

Caroline took a deep breath. "So. Where does that leave us?"

"We need to get the dagger and find out what's so special about it," Lucas said, sitting up. "This dagger is the thing that everything else revolves around. Whoever controls the dagger probably controls the whole situation."

Spark's eyes narrowed. "I'm pretty sure that doesn't logically follow."

"Hey, how about a compromise. We get the dagger, then call Mitch. He's an FPAA forensics lab mage. He can tell us if there's anything hinky about the thing, and then we can figure out what to do from there, okay? Bring in the guys if we need to."

"But—"

"They're not going to arrest you, Lucas," she cut him off. "Not for trying to defend yourself from an organized crime family, even if they're a medium-small sized one."

Lucas glanced at her and his expression was so sad and so tired that she leaned forward to hug him.

"Thanks, C," he sighed into her hair. "Thing is, in my experience, law enforcement looks poorly on stealing, no matter who is doing it, or why. Unless I was working for one of them, of course, and even then there are rules. The advantage of my service is that I skip the rules entirely. And once arrested, my magic would be on record and visible to anyone who looks, which would put a bullseye on my back, even in prison, and not just from bad guys, either. Having one of the world's first technomages under your control is just too valuable a commodity."

"The guys would never do that to you. We couldn't have saved Greg and Spark without you! You keep helping us for no reason at all! Nobody in the FPAA that knows about your magic would say anything to anyone, even if you *did* get arrested, which they wouldn't do."

She felt Lucas smile into her hair and his arm wrapped around her shoulders.

"Before I met them in person, I made peace with the idea that they will likely have to arrest me at some point. They're good people in your office, for the most part, but as we've learned over the past few years, your agency has a lot of rot, too. I trust Darien, Greg, Mitch, and the few others that know about me, but they're still Federal agents, Caroline. And you will be too, when you get your degree."

That sentence carried such sadness that Caroline shivered. It told her that once she graduated and was promoted to full agent, Lucas would fade from her life. He would back away and probably disappear so that he wouldn't have to lie to her and so she couldn't accidentally snatch the truth from his voice.

"Caroline." Spark's voice was quiet but firm. "We'll figure out the future when it's time to. For now, it sounds like you two have decided on a basic plan. We should focus on that."

"It's a terrible plan," Caroline grumbled into Lucas's shoulder.

"Maybe, but it's the best one we've got," he said. "Why don't you pack, if you're going to insist on coming, and I'll look into what's changed in the security situation since Jeff Junior took over."

Spark sighed heavily. "What *is* it with these wannabe evil overlords naming their sons after themselves?"

Caroline was glad for the chance to laugh.

10

"It's weird talking to you guys like this," Caroline grumbled. She was walking around the historic district, mainly near the river, in Wilmington, North Carolina. Dressed as what she actually was–a college student on spring break–she blended in with the Friday morning crowd easily enough as she wandered in seemingly aimless circles near the home and unofficial operations office of one Jeff Calder Jr. Right at that moment, she was on the far side of the grounds, walking through a park with an admittedly lovely view of the river.

"Well, if they are looking for me, it's best not to give them an easy target by walking around there in plain sight, right?" Lucas's voice whispered through the tiny bud in her ear. "Just be glad my magic can make these comfy earbuds work so well. They're not exactly rated for spy stuff."

He was right. She had agreed with him when he proposed this little scouting trip, but still. When they decided to come down here and poke around the Calder mansion to retrieve the dagger and maybe a few clues as to why it was important, she had not expected to spend a day walking around an admittedly scenic riverfront area under the pretense of being a tourist.

And the benefits of knowing a technomage were surprisingly vast. These earbuds were, indeed, tiny and super comfortable, but meant to connect only to a phone, not keep a whole team in contact with each other.

"That's true, these are better than my actual earbuds. And hey. Just be glad that this place is a nice, comfy mansion on a lake and not, say, an underground lab in the middle of nowhere," Spark chimed in. That, of course, was where they had found Spark when they rescued him.

"I've only seen three guards patrolling the waterfront, but they've been pretty easy to find. Not a lot of the tourists or locals here to enjoy the weather wear jackets to hide sidearms," she said.

"I've counted two going back and forth at the front gate. They could be a bit more conspicuous, I suppose, but I don't really see them looking good in neon-colored shirts with 'henchman' lettering." Spark was hanging out on a bench near a very small picnic area squeezed in between some restaurants and the mansion's grounds, sketching. In theory.

"It's true that the security I've seen on their video feeds haven't been very casual about it. I wonder if Junior is getting nervous?"

Caroline was paying so much attention to the chatter in her ear that when her phone buzzed in her pocket, she jumped. Stepping to the side of the path, she leaned against a tree to red the message.

Darien: *Hey, Sunshine. Having a good day?*

Caroline: *Yep! I even had a nap already since my prof cancelled class my only class for today. Spring break started early!*

Technically true. Caroline had slept most of the drive to North Carolina.

Darien: *Nice! Remember, Point wants you to take a real break. No sneaking into the office next week.*

Caroline: *He just wants to keep me away from the paperwork.*

Darien: *He probably wants you to generate less paperwork. Have any plans? You were too stressed about that paper to tell me the other day.*

A jogger pounded by and Caroline hesitated to type anything. Lying to Darien flat out felt all sorts of wrong.

Caroline: *Lucas dropped by last night. Said he had some stuff to do in Wilmington, so I'm going to hang out with him. We talked Spark into coming too. Maybe we can hit the beach like normal college students. But without the getting drunk and in stupid trouble.*

Darien: *When do you head out? What sort of stuff does he have to do?*

She grimaced and looked around the area. Darien didn't really need to know, right?

Caroline: *Lucas stuff. I'm at the beach, D. Focus.*

Darien: *You're going to give me gray hair, you know that? Don't let him drag you into any trouble, okay?*

Darien: *What am I saying, you'll jump in feet first without looking. Try not to get arrested.*

She laughed out loud at that and promised to do her best.

"Guys, Darien was wondering what my plans are for the break. I told him I'm hanging out with Lucas in Wilmington and going to the beach. Think he bought it?" After a moment, she sighed at the silence over her earbud.

"We're going to have him down here by morning, aren't we?" Lucas sounded resigned.

Spark just snickered.

"I mean, maybe not?" Caroline didn't even sound convincing to herself. Spark actually laughed this time.

"We're going to need you to come with us, miss," a

gravelly voice said from right behind her. She turned and assessed the Calder thug who had addressed her, and his partner, who was scanning the area.

"I'm sorry, man. I'm not about to become a spring break statistic. There's not a chance that I'll go anywhere with either of you."

"It really wasn't a request, miss," he said calmly, He brushed his arm against his jacket so that it swung to the side and revealed his gun for a moment. "Now come quietly."

She couldn't stop the smirk if she had been paid to. "I bet that's very intimidating in most situations."

That did get a reaction, as the man's eyebrows twitched higher.

"Miss, you do realize that there are two of us, trained security men, and we're both twice your size. And armed."

She didn't need her gift to hear the surprise in his voice. He fully expected to just walk up to her, look intimidating, and snatch her off the street without any complaint from her. Caroline tried not to smirk.

"Try not to get shot, okay? The whole damn Stonehaven office would take turns killing me," Lucas said. "Spark's on his way, but is trying to make it look casual. Like he'll accidentally stumble across you being assaulted."

"Armed and dangerous. Got it," she agreed. "I'm still not going anywhere with you."

He blinked and glanced over at his partner who seemed to be just as confused.

He took a step closer to her. "Look—"

"Come any closer and I'll start screaming. I'm fairly loud. Not as loud as my roommate, of course, but Julia would have talked you dizzy and left by now, so you should probably be grateful."

"Lady, you've been circling my boss's house for two

hours, and he has every right to want to know why. Now come and talk to him, okay?" he said.

"Son of a... How the hell does anyone know that?" Lucas muttered. There was the sound of rapid typing in her ear.

"I'm almost there, C," Spark said. "Keep him talking and I'll play startled witness. Maybe make him back off."

"If they know she's been circling, they'll know you have, too," Lucas pointed out. "How, though? There are no more cameras in their system. Just the interior ones and the ones at the gates. I've kept eyes on you with some of the street cams and the business security feeds."

"Maybe they do that too? You're not the only hacker in the world, you know," Spark pointed out.

Caroline tried to focus on the bemused goons.

"It's a tourist area. Tourists wander. I told my sister I'd stay in this area, though, in case some thug tried to start something with me. A girl can never be too safe, you know." Caroline grinned at the increasingly frustrated expressions on their faces.

"Just come with us, lady," he said.

"Hey! What's going on here?" Spark's voice called out.

"Just some thugs thinking they're big and bad and can scare girls into going with them," Caroline answered. "Probably human traffickers or something."

The goons both started to sputter and deny that accusation.

"Not cool, man. Why don't you back off?"

"That's it. Frank, you grab that jerk and we'll figure it out later." The goon in front of Caroline closed the distance between them and reached to grab her. It wasn't even a moment later that he was on the ground, face down, with his arm cranked at an angle that would dislocate his shoulder with the slightest pressure.

"Way too easy. Not even worth bragging to Peaches about," she muttered. "He'd just tell me I could have done it better anyway."

A glance up showed Spark frowning at the ground below him, the thug that had headed his way lying at his feet gasping for breath and trying to rub his eyes at the same time.

"Huh. I've never had resistance when I tried to use my magic. Not since I started working with Mitch, anyhow. Weird."

"What should we do with these guys? Call the police?"

Spark shook himself and shrugged. "No idea. You okay?"

"Ugh. Yeah. This guy was nothing compared to the guys Peaches puts me up against. Got anything in that bag that will tie this guy up? We'll just wrap 'em up and leave them."

"Um…" Spark rummaged through his bag for a few minutes.

The thug under her growled. "Who the fuck are you? You're not gonna get far, whoever you are."

Caroline sighed. "I'm a college girl who is more than a bit familiar with people like *you* who try to drag me off the street. So my friends made sure I could keep you assholes from doing that."

"I don't have anything in my bag, but hang on." Spark crouched down beside the guard that he had disabled–she made a note to ask him, after they got away what he'd done to put his goon down. Now, though, he reached out to pull the thug's arms behind his back and held his free hand over the ground. a thin stream of dust and dirt pulled up from the path and wrapped itself around the wrists of the guard. Spark then came over to Caroline and did the same to her goon.

"Well that's a handy trick," she said. "Earth mages are pretty handy to have around." She grinned at him and he shrugged.

"I've only been learning these spells for a year. I'm not that handy yet." He grimaced down at the guard who was now glaring up at him. "I think it's time to go. That spell will wear off pretty quick, and there's something funny about the earth around here."

"Right. Let's go catch a cab or something. I'll call my sister and let her know, too," she said, trying to keep up their cover. "Can I buy you dinner to thank you?"

Spark grinned. "I was starting to get hungry. Dinner would be nice, thanks."

"We'll find you two. Don't get comfortable. My boss owns Wilmington," the goon snarled.

Caroline just rolled her eyes and kept walking until they were well out of sight.

11

It took Caroline and Spark a good half an hour longer than it otherwise would have to get to the hotel suite they were sharing, since they took precautions against being followed. Spark stepped to the side several times and reached out through his earth magic to check for anyone following them, and Caroline was impressed by how far he had come in such a relatively short time.

"Mitch is an amazing teacher, what can I say? I'm still not sure how I didn't know about half my magic for so long, though."

"Human brains are very weird sometimes," Caroline said with a shrug. "We can't figure out where my weird listening skill came from."

They got out of their third taxi, finally close enough to the hotel to start thinking about perhaps calling for some room service.

"Dammit. You guys close?" Lucas's voice sounded frustrated and annoyed.

"A few minutes, yeah," Caroline answered.

"Good. I have to take this phone call. It's my grandfather." The sigh that followed that statement was a wordless prayer for patience.

"Gotcha. Good luck," she said.

Lucas was still on the phone when they walked into the suite.

"No, I understand that you would like great-grandchildren. I'm still not going to marry whatever debutante you wave in front of me and start cranking out kids, though. No. No, Grandfather I am not being disrespectful, but your pressure didn't work on Mom, and it's not going to work on me. What? No. Oh for the…"

Caroline and Spark exchanged glances. Spark kicked his shoes off and patted Lucas on the shoulder on the way past him into the bedroom the boys were sharing.

"No, Grandfather, I won't allow you to arrange a marriage for me. I've already told you, several times and in a number of ways. I don't care how important her family is, or how rich they are. I– No, I–" He took a deep breath and gritted his teeth. "I will not have this conversation with you again. If you persist in trying to marry me off, it will only end with your embarrassment when I explain to the family involved that not only will I not be marrying their daughter but that I have no intentions of marrying at all, ever. It doesn't matter if it's true or not, I will go out of my way to embarrass you. Goodbye."

He stabbed the screen and glared at it until it went dark.

"My parents always tell me that it was so much more satisfying to slam a phone down onto a base." Caroline smirked.

"Very old school," Lucas said, still glaring at the phone. "I bet they're right."

"I think–"

She was cut off by the sound of her own phone ringing. "We seem to be popular today. Hoo boy, it's Greg."

"Hey, Greg!" She aimed for cheerful and cringed at the nearly demented tone she heard instead.

"Hey kitten, what're you up to? Vacation, hmm?" he asked.

"Yep! Just kicking around, hanging out with friends. You know."

"I heard a very funny thing," he said, almost purring. "I heard that you were asking Shakes about a crime family in North Carolina, and now you're *in* North Carolina. Isn't that funny?"

"Well, you know. Stuff comes up and I happen to know people I can ask about it," she shrugged, even though he couldn't see it. "I was curious. And I'm at the beach."

"Mmmm, that's true. And you do like to know everything about everything," he agreed easily enough. "Thing is, I'm curious now. I'm curious to know what you're doing in North Carolina yourself."

She felt her eyes get wide and she frantically waved at Lucas, who just looked at her like she had three heads. "It's spring break, Greg. Lots of college kids go to the beach for spring break."

Lucas must have connected the dots and his own eyes got huge as he sat up straight.

"Mmm hmmm. I don't suppose the two things are at all related, are they? The crime family being based *right there* near your hotel and the sudden, unplanned trip?" Greg purred.

"What? What do you mean?"

"I mean you need to open the door, Caroline."

The knock on the door came immediately after those words and Caroline's head whipped to gape at it.

"C... Is that who I think it is on the other side of the

door?" Lucas's words came slowly, as if he was forcing them out into the air.

She stood and stepped over to the door and looked through the peephole to see not only Greg glaring at her, but Darien as well.

"Shit."

"That is what you're in now, yes." Greg sighed. "Open the door, Caroline." The phone went dead.

She opened the door and sighed. "Hey guys. Can't a girl have a nice beach trip with her friends without you getting all suspicious?"

Darien flopped onto the hotel bed, propping his back with the pillows and crossing his ankles. "She could, sure. If that girl wasn't you and one of the friends involved wasn't just as bad as you are with the shenanigans. I will do my best to save you anytime you're kidnapped, but it's gotten to be more of a habit than we really like. What are you up to, Sunshine?" She heard the worry in his voice, and the hurt that she didn't call him about whatever was going on. Something in her chest twisted.

"You're lucky Point isn't here himself. We told him that you and Lucas were off together and we were nervous, and he just sighed, pinched that spot between his eyes, and sent us after you," Greg said. "You're in a wee bit of trouble, young lady. It takes a lot to give a troll a headache."

Caroline blinked at him for a moment, hearing many of the same feelings in Greg's voice. She hated disappointing her friends. On the other hand...

"I don't need a babysitter, you realize. I am allowed to do things without your supervision, including hang out with my friends."

Darien sighed. "That's true, but is hanging out all you plan to do? Look at him, that eye didn't punch itself." He pointed at Lucas's still healing face. "And he's more of an active trouble magnet than you are. Lucas, I understand that you feel that justice isn't always served via legal methods, but there are better ways to do things."

"In all fairness, I got jumped," Lucas grumbled. He slumped into the chair at the small desk in the room. "I didn't *want* to get yanked into an alley and beaten up."

Greg's eyes snapped over to Lucas. "Explain, please."

So Lucas told him the story of getting jumped by a goon, then finding his house tossed, and the phone call. "I connected a few dots, and now we're here looking into it."

"Why would the the younger Calder be after you?" Darien asked. "What'd you take from them?"

"What makes you think he took something?" Caroline demanded.

Darien just quirked an eyebrow at her. "Really?"

Lucas sighed and grimaced. "Calder Senior's widow asked me to find one of the items her husband left to her in his will. I checked into the will and she wasn't lying about that." He finished speaking with his head up, almost daring Darien and Greg to say something.

"The information we were given says that the widow died as well." Darien frowned.

"She did. 'Tragic car accident.'" Lucas even added air quotes to underline his sarcasm. "I'd be willing to bet that Junior had a hand in it. That kid's a snake."

"He's older than you are," Greg pointed out with a grin.

"Then maybe he should act like an adult?" Lucas shrugged. "Anyway, I had already acquired the thing, and stashed it somewhere safe until it was time to hand it over. But then my client was dead and things were feeling very sketchy, so I ducked out."

"And how did they find you again now?" Darien asked.

"I'm not completely sure, to be honest. Either the Widow Calder wrote things down in a journal or something, or..."

"Or maybe Lynn let it slip," Caroline jumped in. "Lynn Graves, cousin to Jeffery Calder Junior, and apparently beloved niece. She was close to her aunt, and was with her through hiring Lucas."

Darien sat up. "And how does Lynn Graves fit in?"

"She called my work line in a panic yesterday when the FBI agent she thought she was meeting turned out to be one of her cousin's thugs. She doesn't trust Jeff, and is getting increasingly concerned for her own safety. She was hoping we could tell her where the dagger was so she could use it as leverage or something," Lucas said. "To be fair, I was a bit knocked around so I don't remember the whole conversation as well as I wish I did."

"I don't trust her," Caroline added. "I didn't get the sense that she was anything other than honest, but..." She made a face and shook her head. "There was something off about her."

"You're just jealous," Lucas said, grinning. "You're used to being the cutest girl in the investigation, and she was competition for about two minutes."

"Wait, you saw her in person?" Greg leaned forward. "I thought you didn't do in-person meetings."

"Well, yes. Under normal circumstances that's true. But this is hardly a normal circumstance. And I do make exceptions for cases involving real fear and innocents."

"Lynn Graves is part of the Calder crime family. Innocent isn't a word I would use to describe her," Darien said.

Lucas shook his head. "She knows about her cousin, and her uncle before him, but she herself isn't involved. She's trying to run her businesses honestly and intended to talk to the Feds about her cousin's activities when her aunt died, but hasn't been able to meet with her contact yet thanks to Junior."

Darien looked unconvinced, and was about to say something when the door between the rooms opened and Spark came back. His hair was still damp and he had a pizza delivery menu in his hand.

"Oh, hey guys. I was just thinking pizza for dinner. Any objections?"

"Ooh, yes please!" Greg bounced up to peer at the menu over Spark's shoulder.

"I could eat," Darien agreed.

"Wait, you're not surprised to see them, are you?" Caroline glared at him. "We agreed that we weren't going to do anything to get Lucas arrested."

Spark snorted. "Okay, first off, nobody's here to arrest Lucas, are you guys?"

Darien rolled his eyes. "No."

Greg laughed. "Not this time. Probably." He winked at Lucas.

"Second, I didn't have to call them down here. They were halfway to figuring out your little plan well before I told Greg that I was down here with you. Oh, and I figured out how those security thugs knew you were around without having cameras and whatever."

"Excuse me, security thugs? The hell are you up to, Sunshine?" Darien narrowed his eyes at her.

So she just sighed and gave them a short explanation of what they had been doing that morning. Darien groaned and flopped back on the bed at the end of the tale.

"How do you get yourself *into* these messes? Armed thugs? Seriously, Caroline?"

"Peaches would never let me hear the end of it if I had

let those guys touch me," she protested. "I barely even had to do anything to put him on the ground."

"Peaches wouldn't have let you get into the situation in the first place," Darien pointed out.

A sharp whistle cut through their bickering before it could really gain steam, and they all turned to look at Lucas.

"We get it, Darien. Believe me, we get it," Lucas said once he had their attention. "Spark, what did you figure out? They don't have any sort of cameras or anything past the property fence, I've triple checked, just since you got back. There's nothing."

"There's nothing *technological*," Spark corrected him. "There's a lot of magic though. I'm still learning about how to harness my earth magic and how to tap into that power to fuel the fire spells Aldebrand was so pissed about because I couldn't do them the way he did. But, I have learned a hell of a lot of theory, thanks to Mitch and the tutors he's found for me."

"So, they have some sort of wards up or something?" Lucas asked with a frown.

"No," Spark said, shaking his head. "Not wards. They've got either an earth mage or an air mage monitoring the people in the area. I was feeling a faint tingle of magic the whole time I was on the bench, but I didn't really think about it much since it never changed or *did* anything. It was like something nearby was enchanted or maybe there was a low-level spell running in one of the shops, but I'd bet it was a monitoring spell."

"So you weren't a threat since you were pretty much stationary the whole time you were there watching," Caroline nodded. "If they did send someone to check on you, you were sketching, and it made sense."

"And what were you doing, kitten?" Greg asked.

She shrugged. "Wandering around. Counting guards. Stuff like that."

"So, basically being suspicious as hell. Got it." Darian sighed.

"Hey!"

"Okay, so now that the cavalry has arrived, what's the plan?" Spark cut through the squabbles quickly. "After I order the pizza, I mean."

"I'm going after the dagger," Lucas said.

"Um, no?" Caroline couldn't get past the magical sensors. "If they're monitoring with magic they'll know the second you set foot anywhere near that mansion.

"Dagger's not in the mansion." Lucas grinned.

"Wait, what? Why were we counting guards and all that, then?"

"It's nearby. Just not actually on the property," Lucas said.

"So, what you're effectively saying is that your plan is to go retrieve stolen property, and you're informing two and a half Federal agents before you head out." Darien tipped his head in thought. "Yeah, okay. That sounds entirely reasonable. Do you actually *want* to get arrested?"

"Look, whatever's going on, we need leverage. You can't go storm the house all FPAA-raid-style because you have no evidence. No case, even. Once I have the dagger I can turn it over to Mitch or whoever and they can figure out what's so damn special about it."

"There's still no case against Calder, and we have no reason to handle stolen property aside from using it as evidence in a theft case!" Darien pointed out. "We have no reason to be here."

"How about assault and battery, and attempted kidnapping. Is that a case?" Lucas pointed at the bruise on his face.

Darien sighed and Greg peered at Lucas, going so far as to step over to him and tip his head to bring the bruise into the light better.

Darien sighed. "Let me make a few phone calls."

12

Just as Darien was dialing whoever—probably Point—and Greg stepped over to the connecting door to follow Spark, yet another phone rang in the room. Caroline watched Lucas dig his burner "work" phone out of his pocket and wondered if it was just phone call hour.

"Hello? Oh, hi, Lynn." Lucas glanced at Caroline and made a face. "Well, yes, we're here, but we've found a slight stumbling block. Yes. Do you know if your cousin has any new security around the mansion?" He nodded a few times and slumped back to stare at the ceiling while he listened. "I see. Has he hired any mages or that sort of thing? Uh-huh. Huh, okay."

Caroline sat back on the sofa and tried not to eavesdrop on either conversation. It was tough though. Lucas was basically throwing the whole conversation out in his voice, and her talents were latching onto it. Lynn wanted an update on what was going on. Lucas thought she sounded anxious on the phone but calm for now. Still, they had only left her at her hotel in Stonehaven a little under twenty-four-hours ago. Lucas was tired and stressed, and trying to be calm and supportive for Lynn but was also more than a little anxious for himself as well. Lucas stood up and started pacing slowly across the room from his table by the window all the way to the door and back, his path taking him past Caroline's knees as he stepped between the sofa and the beds.

Darien, on the other hand, *was* calm. Irritated, yes, but focused. He was talking to someone about ongoing investigations and who was around the mansion right now. He also wanted to know any information gathered regarding the current state of Calder's security teams and how far out from the property they watch.

Did they bring a first aid kit? Caroline felt like she had a headache coming on from all the information she had magically hitting her now.

"Okay, Lynn. I'll call you with any updates. Okay. Stay safe, now. Bye." Lucas groaned and turned to flop over onto the sofa.

"Gonna make it there, Lucas?" she asked.

"Give me one good reason not to run away to Maui right now," he said without looking up. "I can sell my house, and take up professional beach bumming."

Caroline laughed. "Why?"

"Because this week is going to kill me," Lucas sighed dramatically. "My grandfather wants to arrange a marriage for me. A nice girl from a nice family, he said. Which means some poor, browbeaten girl that is probably just barely legal, who can't or won't tell her misogynistic parents to stuff it. She is, naturally, from a wealthy, *respectable* family, and is probably expecting to get married off, pop out a bunch of kids, then spend her life as a suitable decoration for her husband and sons."

"Um, wow. People still do that?" Caroline couldn't even

begin to imagine her parents trying to arrange a marriage for her.

Lucas groaned and rubbed his hands over his face. "Yes. People definitely still do that," he said. Then hs sighed and scrunched up his face. "I really shouldn't judge. I know a few couples who were arranged, and they actually seem perfectly happy. Hell, one couple I know, the wife is the CEO of a fairly successful local chain of hardware stores while her husband paints. They're a little stupid for each other. It's sweet."

Caroline chewed on her lip while he spoke, hearing his distaste for the practice even as he voiced his very mild support for his acquaintances. The idea of Lucas getting married—at all, but especially to someone he didn't choose himself—made her stomach sour.

"I assume that's not the sort of woman your grandfather is looking for, though?"

"Lord no. He's very *traditional*," he said, physically making air quotes around the word. "By which I mean he's a misogynistic, controlling bastard who thinks he's some sort of grand Family Patriarch, and still hasn't forgiven his daughter for running off and eloping with her firmly middle-class *white* college sweetheart. He only started speaking to her again when she delivered a bouncing baby boy. He came to the States from India when he was barely an adult himself. Some sort of family drama that he won't talk about. Just mutters sometimes under his breath. As far as I can tell, he and his older brother got into it, and Grandfather had to leave or something."

"That's…wow."

"Yeah. He was mostly okay when I was a kid. We didn't spend a ton of time around him though. Mom knew her dad well enough to not want me exposed to him too much, even though she loved him." He sighed again. "So he's trying to set me up with a match like he would have Mom. He wants to leave some sort of family dynasty or something, I don't even pretend to understand it. He's mad because I'm not already a respectably powerful mage, by his standards, or working in some prestigious profession. It's painfully stereotypical. I ought to be a doctor, you know, though a lawyer or politician would be acceptable to him as well."

"Good grief. You and Spark. You're a stupidly powerful mage, Lucas. I mean, you told us yourself there are only a couple more technomages out there," she said. "Isn't that prestigious enough?"

"Oh, he doesn't know. Oh lord, he can *never* find out. It would be on the front page of every newspaper everywhere and I'd be married off to some meek socialite heiress and studied under a microscope by the government, assuming I'm even allowed to live freely at all. The damn fool only sees how he can get status out of a thing, not how it might affect anyone else, let alone me."

"Wow."

"Yeah. When I started showing signs of my particular specialty, Mom and Dad sat me down and really drilled it into my head not to let anyone know. I had to be very *very* careful of using my talents anywhere outside the house." Lucas finally grinned. "I watched you guys for a long time before I told you. I, um, sort of bugged your cars. And tapped your phones. And followed your cases."

"You jerk!" Caroline punched his shoulder. "I can't believe you!"

"Well, I had to know for sure that if you found out none of you would, well, let the government do to me what Aldebrand wanted to do to Greg." Lucas shrugged. "I'm easily as valuable as he is, considering how much the world relies on technology and the internet. It's the one place everyone can feel safe from mages and other things that magically go bump in the night. I could get into any of that and do some very serious damage if I chose to. Knowing that literally everything is vulnerable to me and my magic..."

Lucas wasn't bragging. He was being completely honest with her, and she could hear it in his words. He was, very likely, the most powerful person she would ever meet, and he chose to use that power looking for missing college students and returning ancient artifacts to the country they were stolen from. He barely murmured a complaint when he stayed up for days helping them track down Greg and Spark last year, even though showing his power might have gotten him locked up in a lab somewhere himself.

Caroline blinked in shock. Holy shit, that's why Point let Lucas wander in and out of the office almost at will. He was keeping Lucas close, letting Mitch and a few select others study Lucas and his powers without keeping him a prisoner. Point wasn't *putting up* with Lucas, Point was *protecting* Lucas.

She really needed to buy that grumpy troll some flowers.

"Anyway. Grandfather called to tell me he found me a nice girl to marry and I should start getting ready for the wedding, don't worry he'll arrange everything," Lucas said, letting his head flop back on the sofa cushions again. "I've told him repeatedly that I'm not doing it, but he keeps trying."

"Lame. Where is he?"

"Nursing home, thank god. Which sounds horrible for me to say, but he's getting the care he needs and he's out of my hair usually. When I was in college he had a massive stroke. He needed full-time care for a long time while he recovered, and either I came home to do that myself or he went into a home. I won my freedom by pointing out how bad it would look for me to drop out of school within a year of graduation." Lucas grinned wickedly. "Once he was there, I managed to convince him to stay by pointing out all the 'servants' he had at his beck and call."

"Servants?" Caroline's eyebrows pinched together a bit.

"That's what he calls the nurses and staff," Lucas said, rolling his eyes. "And there were several ladies there as well, for the old goat to hit on. He's not in the full-time care area anymore, he's got a small apartment and all that, but he has his life and I have mine."

"And you didn't need any of his nonsense when you were already dealing with being beaten up by crime family thugs," she said, nodding. "I can understand that."

"Yeah. Pressure I don't need. And then Lynn calls wanting to know if we've got the dagger yet, is it over yet, can she go home yet, all that stuff. And all that after you were assaulted this morning?"

Caroline laughed. "I may have been assaulted, but the battery was all my doing. And Spark's. Those goons are rethinking what an easy target looks like this afternoon."

Lucas chuckled. "True enough. And then these two showed up... I just need an hour or so without major surprises, please?" He sighed. "I have some spells out looking for more information on how those goons even knew you were there, and who all is in the mansion these days. I'm looking into the cousin too. The one that's supposed to be interested in taking over from Junior? Lynn sent me an email with some information about the guy, since he is also *her* cousin, and he sounds like a real peach."

"Lovely."

Caroline slid down until her head was resting on Lucas's shoulder, and he leaned his cheek onto the top of her head, and they sat there for a long moment, letting the sounds of Darien talking on the phone and Greg and Spark's muted voices from the next room wash over them.

"So what do we do, then?" Caroline asked.

"Get the dagger, figure out why they want it so badly, then make a plan," Lucas said. He moved slightly under her head and she guessed he had started to shrug, but held off. Maybe he was still too sore. "Once we have the thing that everyone seems to want, we can decide what to do with it. Maybe we can even set a trap or something and your guys can arrest these jerks, get them out of everyone's hair."

Caroline hummed. It wasn't a great plan. It barely even qualified as a plan, really, but if Jeff Calder was going to be sending goons after Lucas and Lynn Graves, then they had to figure out a way to make him stop. Getting hands on this dagger seemed to be the only option available.

Unless Darien was coming up with a better plan with whoever he was talking to. Caroline's overactive talent had blessedly calmed down and now his voice had faded into the background a bit without forcing her to hear his meanings and emotions.

The line between gift and curse could be damned thin.

"I don't think that's much of a plan, Lucas."

"Maybe not, but it's the plan I've got."

13

Darien was still on the phone, probably with Point, Caroline figured, and Greg had come back into the room and was now discussing pizza toppings with Lucas back at the table. The great pineapple debate raged on. Caroline wasn't sure whether she was glad to see the guys or not. They were absolutely the people she wanted around if things hit the fan, and lord knew it was more than possible with this situation, but for some reason, she didn't want them there.

Her phone rang, distracting her from the puzzle.

"Hey Mom."

"Hey, sweetie. How's school?"

"Good. I turned in my last paper until finals, and I think it came out okay. Mitch from work helped me out a bit." Caroline sighed.

Greg pulled a couple of stress balls from his pocket and started them flashing through the air as he juggled. Spark stepped back into the room rubbing his fingers through his hair, still damp from his shower, and grinned at the sight before flopping onto the small sofa beside Caroline.

"That's great! Sounds like you're knocking this semester out of the park again!" Her mom was definitely one of her biggest cheerleaders.

"I'm trying. How're you guys?"

"Oh, you know. Your dad twisted his ankle last weekend, bowling of all things," Mom said. "Now he's staying on the sofa and moaning about it, and trying to get me to wait on him hand and foot because he's *wounded*. It was cute for the first day, but now I just wish he'd grab a bandage and get on with it. Gerald has been coming over from next door and helping us out a bit with the heavy things Dad can't do while he 'heals from his great injury.'" Mom laughed. "He's such a sweet boy, says to say hi when we talk to you, and I think he's brought Mr. Olaffson right back to life. He still complains about everything, but now it's more like he's playing the part instead of genuinely unhappy. Having Gerald around to help him out has just brightened the whole street! Renting that boy a room was the best decision the old coot's ever made."

"That's great, Mom. I knew that situation would work out." Caroline smiled. Mr. Olaffson had thought he was being watched over by his daughter's ghost one Christmas when Caroline had been home visiting. It turned out to be Gerald, a homeless brownie, who was hiding from the worst of winter behind some boxes in the old man's basement and was repaying him by doing chores and helping out around the house. Finding him and making the whole situation official and aboveboard was one of Caroline's proudest moments. "Gerald's a sweetheart, tell him I said hi back."

"Oh! I saw that Maureen girl from your high school the other day! She was with some of the other girls from your class and said they were on spring break, and I thought yours must be coming up soon, isn't it?"

"Yeah, Mom. It's right now, in fact. I'm in North Carolina with the guys. I spent the morning hanging out in the Historic District of Wilmington and we're debating the beach for tomorrow." Sort of.

"Oh." And the disappointment in her mother's voice was exactly why Caroline hadn't brought it up. "Well, tell them I said hello! I'm so glad you have such good friends. The way you talk about them, It's like you have family with you. It makes me feel so much better about you being out there on your own. I wish you could come back to visit, though."

"I was just there a few months ago, and I'll be coming out the end of June, remember? I just..." Caroline sighed deeply, and Spark turned to raise an eyebrow at her in question. "It's time for me to stand on my own, you know? I know I'm just a college student, but I can't rely on everyone else to lead me through everything forever."

Whatever reaction she was expecting from her mother, chuckling was not it. "Sweetie, you're one of the most stubbornly independent people I have ever known. There's no shame in seeing your family, or in leaning on us if you need it. That includes your found family out there, I would like to point out. And if you could find a nice boy to date, even better."

Caroline blinked. "Um, okay? And I know I can lean on you guys if I need to."

Mom laughed out loud this time. "No, you really don't, but that's okay. I know that Darien and Greg and all won't let you get into too much trouble with that headstrong independent streak of yours. You tell them I'm thinking of them, okay, and I'll let you go. Sounds like you've got plenty to do. But do come visit soon? We miss you."

"Yes, Mom. I love you guys."

Her mom chuckled and let Caroline off the phone. Caroline looked up to see Spark frowning at his soda can.

"Hey, you okay?"

Spark glanced up and flashed a small smile at her. "Yeah. I'm okay. I just..." He shrugged after a moment. "I just never had that so it's strange sometimes. Hearing someone talk to their parents."

"Oh." Caroline heard the ache in his words and the longing for family. When she had first laid eyes on him, he was screaming in rage and pain, his magic flowing out of him to shake the very earth around them, and in that moment her gift had shown her flashes of his childhood. Caroline, more than any of them, knew how isolated and beaten down he was kept by the man who fathered him. The few people he remembered fondly were servants, and even they weren't able to do much.

"Yeah, it's not a big deal. I didn't mean to eavesdrop or anything, sorry."

"No, Spark. If I'd wanted privacy I'd have left the room. It's fine. And wait till you meet them. Mom'll adopt you in about three seconds." Caroline grinned. She reached over and dragged him into a hug, too. "And Mom also reminded me that found family counts just as much as blood. We're your family, Spark. You're not alone anymore."

He put his head down on her shoulder and hugged her back for a few minutes.

"Thanks," he mumbled into her shoulder.

"Anything for one of my irritating new brothers," she said with a grin.

Spark just snorted a laugh and sat up. His eyes were suspiciously shiny, but he grinned back at her.

"Wait a second…" Caroline peered at him, and he blinked back at her, all innocence. "You! You told them what we were doing, even after all that discussion about it! You called them anyway!"

"I didn't call anyone!" Spark said, opening his eyes wide in an attempt to look even more innocent of anything at all.

"Lies! Falsehoods! Shenanigans! You told Greg!" Caroline accused. Lucas and Greg started laughing from where they sat and she looked over at Darien who was smirking, but still on the phone.

"He may have asked what I was up to this morning, and what was I going to do, lie to him? I would never!" Spark sat up straight and tried to look earnest.

Caroline grabbed a pillow from behind her and lunged at him with it. "You're a menace! You really are a brother, aren't you, you tattletale!"

After a few minutes of wrestling, she managed, at last, to pin him down. Okay, so it looked a lot like sitting on his arms and smooshing him back into the sofa, but she'd take the win. Everyone was laughing now, even Darien, who was finally off the phone.

"You're both right," he said. "You're family, Spark. And yes, Caroline, he told Greg all about you're harebrained scheme to get Lucas out from under this threat. Because he doesn't want to see either of you dead, or worse."

"We were trying to—"

"We know what you were trying to do, C. But when you're under duress and defensive isn't the best time to be making huge decisions." Darien turned to Lucas. "Look. We are all fully aware that you skirt the law, at best, when you're out there playing the shady hero of dubious resources. But there are a few things you didn't take into account. The first thing is that the second you dragged Caroline and Spark into your little scheme, this stopped being about you alone."

Lucas had the good grace to look ashamed of himself, his shoulders slumping.

"You're not stupid, Lucas, despite your best efforts to convince us otherwise," Darien said. "Now. Point has looked into the situation a little, and while there are several agencies keeping an eye on the situation, there are only two active investigations. Not that they're *very* active at the moment, apparently."

"And you three have managed to walk smack into the middle of them," Greg added.

"What does that mean?" Caroline asked.

"Well, one thing it means is that we're going to have to explain who you are to everyone when they want to know who was being hassled by Calder's security guys." Darien sighed. "Point is on that, and you're going to have to be really nice to him for a while, Sunshine. Explaining to other agencies why his people stumbled into their investigations is not his most favorite pastime."

"Point's gonna ground us, isn't he?" Caroline groaned.

"Well, you, maybe." Greg grinned at her. "These two don't actually work for him, after all."

"I might as well move my desk into Peaches's training room." Caroline let herself flop over onto the sofa and flung her arm over her face.

"Well, at least you keep making all *new* dumb mistakes," Darien said. He stood and patted her leg as he walked past to the door. "You can learn. There's hope for you yet. I'm going to go get us some sodas before the food gets here. Any requests?"

14

Caroline slipped into the passenger seat of the rental car and looked back at the hotel door. The gray light of pre-dawn softened the building and muted noise, like a blanket still clinging to the edge of a bed. Soon the sun would be fully up and the broad daylight would yank the blankets off the whole city, but for the moment, Wilmington slept on.

More importantly, Darien, Greg, and Spark slept on.

They had spent the rest of yesterday afternoon and well into the night discussing plans and plots and possibilities, and had ended up with no new ideas at all. And while they didn't exactly have a ticking clock as far as Calder was concerned—at least not as far as she knew—she and Spark did need to be back in class next week. And it would be very nice not to spend the entire break chasing down hidden treasures.

"Are you sure about this?" she asked.

Lucas slid into the driver's seat and glanced at her as he started the engine. "Nope," he said with a lazy shrug. "But after the planning session yesterday I get the distinct feeling that if we don't just do it, those three will talk us into a hole. I may not want to be arrested, but I want to be murdered in a back alley even less."

He turned the car onto the road and pointed it back into the city. "Besides, they can't get *too* angry. They don't want us going near the mansion, and we're not." He grinned. "Relatively speaking."

Caroline sighed. Lucas wasn't lying. Wherever they were heading was near the Calder mansion, but not as close as they had been yesterday. "It would probably have helped if you had told us where you stashed the damn dagger in the first place. Why check the security if we're not going in?"

"Because we needed to know how alert they are, and if they're looking for me in town." Lucas wasn't grinning anymore. "Turns out that they are on high alert and they know that *someone* is in town. They suspect it's me, according to the emails I read yesterday. Junior is very upset and wants me brought to him, presumably for beating and interrogation, the short-sighted thug. I wonder if the thought of paying me off even occurred to him."

Caroline huffed out a laugh and looked out her window at the city whooshing past. The light was brighter now, though still gray. The sun held dawn just barely below the horizon. Maybe in a day or two she could sit on the beach and watch the sunrise over the ocean instead of chase after a stolen magic artifact. Again.

"I am too young to be this exhausted at the thought of my job," she grumbled.

Lucas chuckled. "Well, with you it does seem to be either piles of paperwork or active disasters."

"What are you trying to say, Mr. Chased-by-mobsters?"

Lucas laughed outright this time. "Nothing in particular. Just seems to be feast or famine with you on the excitement front. I'd be exhausted, too."

Caroline sighed. "Where are we going?"

"We are going to a very neat little pirate museum, and then we are going to get breakfast." Lucas grinned. "Do you like pirates?"

Caroline blinked. "Pirates?"

"Yeah. Did you know Edward Teach, the notorious pirate Blackbeard sailed these very waters?" Lucas asked. He waved vaguely toward the ocean as he turned the car into a parking lot. Caroline glanced up at a low-slung building topped by a carved wooden sign featuring a skull and crossbones at the top and the words "Wilmington Pirate Museum" underneath in bright red paint. "I figured we'd pick up the dagger, then get some breakfast to go and take it back to the guys. If that's okay."

"That's where you hid the dagger? A pirate museum?" Caroline couldn't hide her amusement.

"What better place for an artifact than a museum?"

"What, you just stuck it in an exhibit?" She laughed.

Lucas grinned at her and didn't say anything.

"Oh my god, you just stuck it in an exhibit. All those rich and powerful crime families and their many minions freaking out and searching everywhere and beating you up and the whole time it's been sitting in there with a damn pirate mannequin and a chest full of fake treasures?"

Lucas's smile turned downright evil. "Pretty much."

Caroline heard the satisfaction in his words. "How can you be so smug about that? You got the shit kicked out of you! You're lucky you only came out of that with some bruises! Lucas!"

His smile faded.

"I know." His fingers brushed over the still-purple skin of his face. "But it's better that I carry this sort of burden than some innocent. If those guys get their hands on this dagger, I don't know what sort of power it has, but I know that it won't be rainbows and sunshine if Calder gets it. He's petty and reckless and greedy for power. His father was, at least, level-headed and deliberate in his criminality. He may have committed illegal acts and pulled the strings of power behind the scenes, but he wasn't spreading violence out in the streets. Since Junior took over the violent crime rate in the areas he controls has tripled. There were signs of it even when i took the job in the first place, which is why I didn't just leave it around for him to find again when my client turned up dead."

"So you know that Calder Junior is a violent thug and you still thought to what, tweak his nose by smugly putting this thing he wants in the most ridiculous place you can think of?" Caroline demanded.

"No. But I didn't want to have the thing on me, in case this exact thing happened," Lucas sighed. He drove his fingers through his hair, making it stand up and look a little wild. "I was careful, but it's always a possibility that someone could put the clues together to figure out who stole their precious whatever. Junior doesn't care who he destroys as long as he gets richer and more powerful in the process. I don't know what's so important about this damn knife, but the fact that he wants it so badly is enough of a reason for me to keep it away from him. He's already doing serious harm to the community, but who knows what he'd do if he gets this thing. It could be enchanted to give him some sort of power or to kill his enemies from a distance. My safety isn't important compared to that."

Caroline seethed. "And what about those of us that care about you, you jerk?" She hit his arm, smacking his bicep hard. "If you'd been killed in that alley, what about us? Were not important? The fact that we were already worried about you disappearing just before you turned up in Stonehaven isn't important?"

"That's why I showed up there, mostly. I knew you'd worry if I didn't get in touch eventually," Lucas said.

"*I* would worry? *Darien* was wondering why we hadn't heard from you." Caroline smacked him again. She felt a flicker of satisfaction when he winced and rubbed his arm. "*He's* the one that prompted me to text you. You have *friends*, you jackass! Spark's right. You have allies, goddamn *call us* when you need help!"

Lucas's jaw flexed and his mouth opened and closed a few times, like he was trying to speak but his voice wasn't cooperating. He finally licked his lips and nodded. "Okay."

Caroline glared at him. "You're already in the doghouse, buddy. Don't screw up like that again."

The corner of Lucas's lip twitched now, but he swallowed and nodded. "Yes, ma'am."

"Damn right."

She turned back to look over the building and took a deep breath. "So. What's the plan?"

Lucas twisted in his seat and reached into the back to pull his tablet out from his satchel. A few taps and images from inside the building popped up.

"The place doesn't open until ten. Staff starts arriving at eight, so we have about forty minutes now to get in there and snatch the dagger. It's in this display." He tapped one of the small squares of video feed and it suddenly filled the screen. A pair of pirates were frozen mid-battle, swords crossed, one reaching for the pistol tucked at his waist while a small group of three more cheered at the side near a stack of crates and a chest. Naturally, the chest was thrown open to reveal the pile of treasure inside.

"See there?" He pointed at a corner of the pile of loose

coins and jewels. The edge of a hilt seemed to poke out, obscured mostly by two strands of pearls draped over it.

"When you hide something in plain sight, you don't kid around," Caroline said.

"Why thank you!" Lucas grinned. "You sit here and keep an eye on the cameras. Let me know if you see anyone coming. I'm going to go in and grab the dagger. I'll be back out in ten minutes and we'll go get breakfast. Promise."

"Lucas..."

"It's not like this place is swarming with mobsters or henchmen or anything. I can dodge a few curators and a janitor if they come in early. But I have to hurry now," Lucas said. He handed her the tablet, now showing all the camera feeds again. "You can scroll through them like this."

After a minute of explaining how to control everything, he handed her an ear bud and, with a cheeky grin, hopped out of the car. Caroline watched him stroll across the parking lot toward the side door, totally calm, like he was wandering down to the corner store for a soda. A moment later he appeared on the tablet screen and waved at the camera.

"Dammit, *Robin*," she growled, using the code name he picked for himself who knew how long ago. "Take this seriously, would you?"

"I am, *Sunshine*," he answered. "I admit I am a better hacker than I am a thief, but this isn't my first expedition. And electronic locks are so much easier."

Caroline growled softly, but just watched as he moved through the screen. A sound nearby had her tearing her attention away from the tablet. A car was pulling into the parking lot. The man who got out was dressed in business casual, and his hair stuck up everywhere as if he forgot to comb it. He juggled a satchel and a shopping bag and a small insulated lunch bag, and sort of fumbled his way to the building, disappearing through the same door Lucas had.

"Robin, you've got company," she said. "Looks like a curator or an admin."

"Aye aye," Lucas said softly before saluting the closest camera.

"Jerk," she muttered. She kept her eyes glued to the screen as she watched him duck and dodge his way past the curator, who seemed to be doing his own walk-through of the building. The man checked in every display and room at least twice, and Lucas had to hide behind the bar in a raucous tavern brawl diorama to avoid detection.

At last, he made it to the treasure chest and carefully extracted the dagger from under the plastic coins and fake pearls. He shifted the plaster pirates' loot around a bit to cover the dagger's disappearance, then dodged back to the door. Caroline swore she didn't breathe until he was halfway back to the car.

"See? No worries" Lucas said as he slid into the driver's seat. He took the tablet out of her hands and then gently replaced it with a dagger.

She frowned at it as Lucas started the car. Plain gray steel shined dully in the early morning light. Around ten inches long, she guessed, it had only a few lines etched into it near the small crossguard but they were faint, almost worn off with age. The handle was just plain, worn leather and the small pommel was a simple round end to finish it off. Both the edges had been dulled by time and lack of care. There was nothing special or interesting about this dagger other than its presumed age.

"I don't get it," she said.

"Me neither. Nothing I've dug up has indicated it's

anything more than a plain antique dagger. Valuable enough for that, but otherwise..." Lucas shrugged. "There's a slight tingle of magic when I pick it up, but nothing big. Maybe not even a whole spell. They do degrade over time, you know, if they're not used."

Caroline was about to speak again when their earbuds crackled to life.

"Where the hell are you two?" Darien's voice demanded.

Lucas laughed out loud. "Relax, big brother. We're getting breakfast. Are you more of a bacon and eggs sort of guy or are you more interested in doughnuts? Or should I pick up a pint of O positive?"

Caroline smacked Lucas's arm as Darien growled in their ears. "Coffee."

"Yessir!" Lucas said. "I'd salute but I'm driving."

Another growl filtered through the earbuds and Lucas laughed out loud.

15

Lucas dropped something on the coffee table in front of Caroline with a clunk and moved past her to slump at his computer. He had taken Greg this time, claiming to want the man's opinion on lunch options. Greg called through the door to get Spark's attention as he sat on the corner of the bed and started rustling through the paper bags he carried.

"That smells amazing." Darien sat up and scooted over next to the blond shifter. Caroline grinned and thought she might never get tired of the contrast. Darien was slim and dark and a little sarcastic beside Greg, who was nearly the poster boy for a blond All-American boy. If he had been human and gone to high school, she had no doubt he would have played football and been prom king. That they both used their looks to hide their badassery added another layer of amusement to her thoughts.

"What did you guys get?" Darien asked, peering over Greg's shoulder.

"Food truck Indian food. Got you some chicken tikka, D."

"Samosas are acceptable," Lucas grumbled from his desk. "Not as good as Mom's, but how could they be?"

"I mean, 'as good as Mom's' is usually an impossible standard," Darien pointed out.

"That's fair," Lucas said.

Caroline frowned at him. "You okay?" She reached out and pulled the mystery package over to look. The rolled-up plastic bag opened to reveal a simple brown leather sheath, worn at the edges and in need of cleaning.

Lucas grimaced then forced a small smile to his face. "I will be. Grandfather called again while we were in line."

She didn't often put effort into using her abilities when she wasn't facing a suspect, but Lucas's smile was far too fake for her not to worry. "What did he want?"

A shrug. "Same thing, different day. He's found a 'very respectable girl' for me. At least this time he proved that he does occasionally listen. This one is, apparently, 'very American. Went to college and everything! And her family is very well respected, she is perfect for you!'" The last words were said in what seemed to be a heavily sarcastic imitation of his grandfather's speech patterns. "He goes through cycles of being really intense about getting me married off, then he backs off for a while. Then it all starts over again."

Caroline heard the frustration and resentment over his grandfather's actions, and the love Lucas still held for the man despite them. There was also pain from his broken relationship with him. She even got a flash of a memory from when Lucas's parents had still been alive. Some family function where they all sat around a table, celebrating and eating his mother's food.

"I'm sorry, Lucas," she said. She reached into the bag and pulled out the sheath, turning it over in her hands.

Lucas sighed. "The old man is feeling his age, and I get

that's scary. Especially since he doesn't know what sort of legacy he is leaving the world, or what sort of mark his family will have on it. I can't tell him about my magic because I know he will just use it as a bargaining chip to secure a better marriage for me and more prestige for the family."

Caroline frowned. After the strong emotions of a moment ago, now it seemed like Lucas was reading from a script. There was no emotion behind his words at all. No memories, no hints of meaning. Nothing but his actual voice. It felt like she was watching television.

"When I first started being able to affect electronics, Mom was the first person I told about what I could maybe do and she sat me down and told me to make sure that nobody learned what I could do unless I trusted them completely." Lucas's voice hitched for a moment and Caroline looked up to see him pressing his lips together for a moment. "She especially made sure I knew not to let Grandfather know, or he would spread the news faster than any gossip could, in order to raise the prominence of the family name. Even though Gerard is my father's family name."

Caroline put the sheath down so she could dig the dagger out from under the sofa as he finished speaking. The moment she did, she was hit with a wall of emotion so strong she actually staggered with it.

"Whoa, kitten, what's wrong?" Greg was kneeling beside her in a flash, Darien on her other side.

"I... I'm not sure." She let the men help her back up onto the sofa and shook her head to clear it. "It was..."

"I shouldn't be boring you with my family drama when you're having actual trouble. What is it, C?" Lucas's attention was on her fully, as well. She could hear the worry for her in everyone's voices.

"I think maybe I'm just hungrier than I thought. Pass me some lunch?" she said.

Darien frowned at her, but pulled over one of the bags and started reaching into it. "Let's see. Naan and the samosas in this one." He handed her one of the piping hot dumplings.

She ate, letting the still-concerned tones of her friends wash over her.

"So, now you tricked me into being your muscle so you could fetch the sheath—"

"Oh, come on. You thought the tour of the battleship was cool," Lucas laughed.

"Well, of course, I did!" Greg protested. "The North Carolina is really cool! Darien, did you know there's a whole battleship here that you can just go take a tour of?"

"I did, in fact. I toured it a few years back when I came here on vacation. *Real* vacation." Darien narrowed his gaze at Caroline and she just shrugged.

"It was probably the last vacation you ever took," she replied primly.

"Well, it was before I got assigned to babysit reckless college interns." Darien nodded as if in serious contemplation. "I've been busy since then."

"Reckless? I'll show you reckless." She threw a couch pillow at him, barely missing when he ducked. The cushion landed on the floor after bouncing off Lucas's knee.

"Hey! Watch the friendly fire!" he protested, laughing.

"As I was saying, children," Greg continued, laugher in his own voice. "I'm not your private security, Lucas."

Lucas scoffed. "I know that, thanks. I've managed fine on my own for years. I just thought you'd like to see the ship, that's all. The fact that I happen to have hidden the sheath in the visitor center building is utterly irrelevant."

"Uh-huh," Spark said, finally joining the conversation. "It wasn't at *all* because you wanted to avoid another purple bruise all over your pretty face."

"You think I'm pretty?" Lucas perked up. "I mean, you're cute, too, Spark, but you're not really my type."

"You're not my type, either, nerd." Spark rolled his eyes. "And you know damn well you're an attractive man, you don't need me inflating your ego any more than it already is. My point is that you want bodyguards when you go out now, so you're drafting us, one at a time."

"Hmm, that does explain why you took Caroline this morning," Darien said nodding slowly. "You knew that she'd let you weasel your way into breaking into the museum for the dagger, but she's also had enough training to handle whoever Calder is likely to send after you. Why hide them in two different places?"

Lucas scoffed. "I thought she would help me pick out breakfast, and wouldn't argue about making a stop. I thought Greg would like the battleship since it's both a cool thing and a piece of history and I know he's into that. And I had no idea if my late client wanted the blade of the sheath. Lord only knows with this sort of people, so I hid them seperately."

"Art history, usually, but yeah, it was cool," Greg agreed.

"So where are you taking me and Darien on our not-bodyguard dates?" Spark batted his eyelashes at Lucas.

Caroline let them bicker and picked up the sheath again. Her sense of her friends cut off immediately.

"Oh, shit." She dropped the leather as if it burned her. It bounced off her knee and came to rest next to the leg of the coffee table.

"What? What is it?" Every eye in the room was watching her now with varying levels of concern.

"That...that sheath. It's..." Caroline did not know a ton about how magic worked. She had listened to Mitch's lectures on the subject and paid attention as much as she could, but considering how surrounded she was by it, it was well out of her understanding. "I can't feel you guys when I'm touching it."

"Feel us?" Spark frowned.

"You mean your empathy-adjacent power?" Darien asked.

"Yeah." She nodded. "When I picked it up, it was like...Like all of a sudden, I wasn't in the room with you, I was watching through a TV. Hell, even then I sometimes get a flicker of something, if the actor or whoever gets really worked up, but..."

God, she had never realized how much she relied on it. It was far from a perfect science, and there was so much left open to interpretation which itself was a skill she was still perfecting. But the sense that people were *there*– real and breathing and feeling and thinking–that was a comfort Caroline had never been aware she needed. The thought that something could take that away was terrifying.

Darien wrapped his arm around her shoulders and pulled her in to lean on him, slowing the shudders that she hadn't even noticed yet. "You're okay, Sunshine. We're here and we're going to figure it out."

"Are you okay now?" Greg asked. "I mean, can you feel us again?"

"Yeah. As soon as I dropped the sheath."

"The sheath is enchanted as well?" Lucas frowned at it where it had tumbled to the floor. "I wonder."

He reached down and picked it up before flicking a finger at the TV. Nothing happened. He tried several more times with a few other electronics scattered around the room. "Damn, that's one hell of a suppression enchantment. I didn't even sense the magic. Anyone else?" Spark and Greg shook their heads and Darien murmured "Nothing."

"Wild," Lucas murmured. "What the hell does this dagger *do* that it needs to be suppressed this hard?" He crouched to reach for the dagger and pulled it from its hiding place. He put them side by side on the coffee table and looked around the room.

"I'm going to head out tonight again to see if I can catch any rumors. The bar I hit last night wasn't quite seedy enough, I think," Darien said.

"I'll hop online and see what research I can do to dig up where this damn thing came from. The magic feels very old. Not medieval, but definitely not from the last century." Lucas said.

"Agreed. This feels old." Spark held his hand over the dagger, then over the sheath. "Man. Now that I know it's there, it's kind of creeping me out. It's like a complete hole in the magic. Think it's as old as the dagger?"

"Could be. It would make sense if whatever the dagger's enchanted to do is that dangerous. Whoever did the enchanting wouldn't want to be destroyed by his own work," Lucas said, moving to look closely at the leather. "You're right, that's creepy as hell. How did I not notice that when I was handling it?"

"No idea. I didn't either. Did you?" Spark glanced at Greg who shook his head.

"I don't sense magic like you guys do. I only really notice it when I'm shifting or using my stealth."

"Same for me," Darien chimed in. "I can only really sense it when I'm drawing on my own magic to use my vampiric speed, things like that. And I don't do that often. Might be that you have to be touching it to be affected. Touching it and actively using magic. Mitch is going to be over the moon when we show that to him. It's stronger than most of our containment devices."

"Safety first," Caroline said. She was trying to shake off the last of the panic that had begun to grip her when her friends, the people in the room with her, had disappeared from her undefined magical senses. "What do we do with the thing?"

"I think a better question is, why does that dagger have a sheath with such a serious dampening spell?" Spark frowned at the bit of leather sitting so innocently on the table. "And why did it affect Caroline?"

16

Greg put the dagger in the sheath, then wrapped them both in a mesh cloth they had borrowed from the containment specialists and stuck the whole bundle in the bottom of his suitcase. Seeing the whole thing disappear into the luggage made Caroline feel a lot better, but the sour residue from her panic still sat heavy in her stomach and her skin felt too tight.

She took a long shower after turning the water up as hot as she could stand it, and scrubbed herself over twice before she started to feel less itchy. How had her weird "empathy-adjacent" talent become such a vital sense to her? She hadn't even noticed it happening, so caught up in wishing it away when she was younger.

It was a problem for another time, maybe. When Lucas was safe and she had a chance to talk it out with someone. There were therapists on staff at the office, both for the agents who needed it–they saw some horrible things in their cases sometimes–and for the victims who needed to be questioned. This seemed like a bigger issue than she should lay on her friends.

When she stepped back out into the room they were now using as their home base, she heard a phone ring.

"Hey, Mitch, hope you have a few minutes, cause we've got questions," Darien said. "I'm putting you on speakerphone."

"Who all is there?" Mitch asked. Darien put the phone on the coffee table and sat back on the sofa. Caroline joined him and tucked her feet under his leg, which earned her a glare with no real heat behind it.

"The usual suspects these days. Greg, Caroline, Lucas are right here, and Spark is wandering in and out.

"Okay, so what trouble have you all gotten into this time?" Mitch asked wryly. "And should I alert Point?"

"Hey!" Caroline protested, but Darien and Greg just laughed.

"Point knows we're here, and I'll call him in a bit with an update. So, here's what we're up to." Darien quickly went over the history of the dagger as they understood it, how Lucas got involved, and the timeline for all the deaths related to it.

"Fascinating. And you don't know why this dagger is supposed to be so important?" Mitch asked.

"Not in the least. Lucas is working on figuring out where Calder Senior got it from but hasn't had a lot of luck yet," Darien said.

"Wherever it came from, he either inherited it or bought it for cash from a less than reputable source. There don't seem to be any records relating to him and buying antiques that aren't of the outrageously expensive and ridiculously gaudy sort," Lucas said.

"So why are you calling me about it?" Mitch asked.

"Well, it's enchanted. To do what, we don't know, but we imagine it's something lethal and cutting-related. Because why else enchant a dagger than to make cutting or stabbing something easier?" Darien said. "Spark and Lucas can both sense *some* sort of enchantment, but whatever it is, it's not obvious," Greg added. He had been lounging on Caroline's bed when she came in but sat up now that Mitch was on the phone.

"Curious, but that doesn't really answer my question. Bring the thing back and I'll run some tests."

"Well, here's the thing. Lucas hid the dagger and the sheath in separate areas," Darien said.

"I could tell that there was an enchantment on the dagger so I hid it in a museum with several layers of security enchantments around it. The bit of display it stayed in was just cheap costume jewelry and other props, but it sat right next to some antique pistols and other weapons, so I figured that the general sense of enchantments in the room would mask the dagger. I didn't even notice the sheath, so I didn't think about it." Lucas scrunched up his face. "I really should have."

"Why?" Mitch's voice was now sharp with interest, and Caroline grinned at Darien. Mitch loved a magical puzzle, and she could sense his growing excitement from his voice, even over the phone.

"Because the sheath is like a goddamn black hole of magic," Spark announced, walking back into the room and perching next to Greg. "And because it affected Caroline when she was just holding it, which let me tell you freaked us all out."

There was dead silence from the phone.

"Mitch? You still there?" Darien leaned over to make sure they were still connected.

"Caroline, tell me exactly what happened," Mitch demanded.

"Um, okay." Caroline did her best to explain what she was doing and thinking the whole time she was handling the sheath. "I mean, I don't get any emotions from people on TV unless it's live and they're feeling really strongly about whatever they're talking about. Sometimes I can pick up when an actor in a movie is using a lot of emotion to get their performance across, but usually, it's just like looking at a photograph. I don't get anything at all, you know?"

"So, like most of the rest of us, then," Darien said gently. He reached out and squeezed her shoulder.

She flashed him a smile and continued. "But that's what holding the sheath felt like. Suddenly, even though I was in the room with everyone and there should have been plenty of information flying around—how honest everyone was being, maybe even flashes of memories, stuff like that—there was nothing. It was like I was watching a video. Then when I dropped it, it all came slamming back."

Mitch hummed. "Why didn't you notice at first? Why did it take so long?"

She shrugged even though Mitch couldn't see her. "Not sure. I've never really understood this talent, let alone controlled it. When I'm not concentrating, it just sort of does its own thing. Gets stronger or weaker or whatever. Around you guys, I'm pretty relaxed. I trust you all, so I don't always pay attention to it, even when it's turned up high. Usually, around people I know really well and trust, it just sort of simmers along and I ignore it. So I think I just wasn't paying attention to it at first, and emotions were pretty neutral."

"But then I started talking about Grandfather," Lucas said slowly. "And you know that I have strong feelings about that whole mess, so you probably unconsciously started trying to look for them."

Caroline nodded and wondered again just how dependent she really was on this skill nobody seemed to understand.

"That seems to be a reasonable theory for now," Mitch agreed. "Now, Lucas and Spark, tell me what you can. Describe this 'black hole' to me."

"It's creepy as hell, Mitch," Spark said. "It's like there is no magic at all around the thing."

"Not even the general background magic in your area?" Mitch asked.

"Not a speck. I just hovered my hand over top of it, and I could almost feel where the magic stopped like a bubble around the thing. Maybe an inch, inch and a half away."

"Did you touch it?"

"Not a chance. I saw how freaked out Caroline was and I could feel the creepy no-magic thing so I wanted nothing to do with it." Spark looked over. "Darien touched it, though."

"But I can't sense magic like you mages can, so it didn't feel particularly different to me. I'd guess it feels like any of the magic containment bags and cloths that we have. I know they make you guys pretty uncomfortable too."

"Yes, they do." They could all hear his shudder over the phone. "Going into the vault is unpleasant, to say the least. Which is why it's mostly shifters and elves that work in there."

"I always wondered about that," Greg mused.

"Lucas, would you agree with Spark's assessment? Do you have anything to add?" Mitch asked.

"I think he covered it. I was a bit on edge when I was hiding the dagger and the sheath, but I assumed that was because of the circumstances. Might have been the containment effect as you called it. What's weird, though, is that I could tell from across the room that the cloth Greg had was a magic dampener, and when I've used them in the past, they were fairly obvious to me. This thing is not. Like, at all."

Mitch hummed again.

"I really want to get my hands on this sheath. This sounds fascinating, and like a huge step forward in containment effects. How soon can you get it here?"

"Hopefully by the end of the week. We have to figure out a way to keep Lucas safe from this Calder goon first," Darien said with a sigh. "Caroline and Spark have class on Monday."

"Tuesday," they corrected him in unison.

"Excuse me." Darien glared at them both in turn while Greg chuckled. "They have class on Tuesday. So no later than that. If we don't have this thing wrapped up by then, I'll send it back with them."

"What about—" Lucas got cut off by Greg clearing his throat. "Okay then."

"So we have two main questions here," Darien said. "First: how does this sheath work? And second: why does the dagger need it?"

"Well, we can run a few quick tests right now, if Spark, Caroline, and Lucas are willing," Mitch said. He ran over a few ideas quickly and Spark volunteered right away. Caroline wasn't sure how she felt about it all, but since she knew beforehand how it would feel, she said that she was cautiously willing to try. Lucas's answer got cut off by his phone ringing. Greg dug back into his luggage, grumbling the whole time about putting things away then taking them right back out.

"Hey, okay, slow down. I can't understand you," Lucas said. He jabbed his finger into his other ear and frowned hard in concentration.

Greg unrolled the package and pulled the dagger out

of the sheath, laying them both on the table. Spark crouched next to the table and peered at the plain worn brown leather.

"Okay, Mitch, I'm ready to go," Spark said. "It doesn't look like much. Some scuffs and wear, but no runes or sigils or anything visible."

"Okay, can you try that small fire summoning we worked on last week? Just hold it in your hand," Mitch instructed.

"Guys, I can't hear, I'm going to step out for a minute," Lucas called from the doorway between the rooms. Caroline glanced up and nodded at him, but her attention was pretty firmly on the sheath and what Spark was doing. He held his hand palm up, and on the surface, a small fireball flickered. About the size of a softball, it glowed warm and bright, the orange flame not burning Spark despite the heat she could feel coming off it.

"Okay, you have it?" Mitch waited until Spark grunted an affirmative.

"Yeah, but it was a little tougher. Like I had to push a bit more than I did last week" Spark said. "Nothing major, though. I'm probably just a bit tired."

"Okay, now hold your other hand above the sheath, but don't touch it. Start from about a foot away," Mitch instructed.

Spark did, and as he continued following Mitch's directions, he watched the fireball shrink and flicker wildly the closer his free hand got to the leather, only to return to normal at just over a foot away, or about where Spark sat.

"I think that's enough to make a reasonable guess. Though if Lucas comes back from his call, I would like him to test it as well. It seems that the sheath is simply a very powerful dampening device. Most such devices are monodirectional. That is, they only dampen enchantments in one direction. Our bags and cloths work that way, for example," Mitch said. "This, however, seems to be more of a bubble in area of effect. The item at the center of the bubble is the most strongly dampened, then the further one gets from there, the weaker the effect."

"Fascinating, but why shield a dagger like that? We haven't noticed anything major about the thing. I can tell it's enchanted, but it doesn't seem all that strong." Spark turned to peer at the knife. "It's pretty plain too. No engraving on the blade to speak of, plain leather wrapping on the handle, it looks like. No gems or extra wire wrapping or anything. Just a plain, lethal-looking dagger. Sharp, though. Looks like it was cleaned recently before Lucas lifted it."

Mitch hummed again. "Bring it to me as soon as you can. I want to take a look. If it has shielding that strong, then it could be dangerous."

"Well, it was on public display for a bit over a year, so maybe it needs to be activated on purpose?" Darien suggested. "I know Lucas was trying to dig up any information on where it came from, how Calder Senior got his hands on it."

"I'll go ask him. He has to be almost done by now," Spark hopped up and went through the door.

"I hope you can get this wrapped up quickly. I don't like the idea of you all down there with a potentially dangerous enchanted weapon and no—"

"Guys!" Spark rushed back into the room, his eyes wide. "Lucas is gone."

17

"Okay, calm down you two." Darien dropped his hand to Caroline's shoulder.

Spark wasn't looking as close to tears as Caroline felt, but his eyes were still wide. Greg stepped up next to the man and rubbed his hand over Spark's back, and the mage visibly relaxed.

"Mitch, I'll call you back. Caroline, call Lucas," Darien instructed.

She was glad he was taking charge because right now she couldn't. After the panic at losing her weird not-magical magic, the realization of just how much she depended on it, and now the loss of her friend, right now was not a good time for her to be planning.

"He's not answering. It's just ringing." She hung up when the voicemail message played, and tried again. The third time she got the voicemail message instructing her to let Lucas know who and what and why, she hung up and shook her head.

"Okay. Greg, you and Spark head outside and see if you can pick up a trail of some kind. I'm going to call

Shakes and see if he can get a bead on Lucas's phone." Darien stood and went to rummage in the mini fridge and came back with a bottle of water, which he handed to Caroline while he waited for Shakes to answer.

"Hey! Yeah, still in North Carolina. Listen, can you track Lucas's phone?"

Caroline drank the water and shook herself back to focus on the moment. This wasn't like her. She wasn't one of those people who freaked out when something happened. She was the sort who, when kidnapped by Elf Supremacists, made an ally of the vampire she was trapped with and got them both out. She tracked down mass murderers who poisoned the blood supply. She broke up human trafficking rings.

She shook off her slide into distracted worrying and forced her brain to focus. They were going to find Lucas.

"Well, Sunshine, Lucas is paranoid enough that he's bespelled his phone to make electronic traces slide off the thing." Darien sighed and sank onto the seat beside her. "You ready to go join the search?"

"Damn right. Let's go."

They carefully locked everything up, and after replacing the dagger in the sheath and wrapping the whole thing back in the containment cloth Greg had, and sticking it not in Greg's luggage, but in the panel in the bathroom that gave access to the plumbing, they headed outside. After a few minutes they caught up with Greg and Spark coming back toward them from across the parking lot.

"He headed toward the street like he was going to walk somewhere, then he got in a car or something. There's a traffic camera, though, that I bet Shakes can get into. Any luck tracing his phone?" Greg asked.

"Nope. Damn technomage has a spell to keep his location untraceable." Darien scowled.

"So, now what do we do?" Spark asked.

"Well, we have a couple of questions we can ask," Caroline answered. Bloody Lucas. "He clearly left on his own. We can assume that something about that phone call inspired him to head out without telling us."

"You mean like he's done twice now, in two days, to retrieve various stolen items?" Darien grumbled.

"Yes. But both of those times he made sure to take one of us for backup. Why would he head out alone now?" Caroline asked. She peered past Greg toward the road. "He cares less what happens to himself than he does about us. He's showed that several times now, but he's not a reckless man. He took us with him to get the dagger and the sheath so that there would be someone there in case he needed help. He took backup, even if he was a sneaky jerk and didn't say so explicitly."

"That's true," Darien agreed. He didn't seem to want to say it out loud, and Caroline heard the irritation at Lucas's cocky attitude as well as worry for the man who had become an ally if not a friend.

"So what do we do? I tried sensing him through the earth, and no luck. But if he's too far away or in a car or something, I wouldn't be able to sense him anyway."

Darien's brows drew together as he thought. "Well, I'd suggest that you two go back to the room, in case the idiot comes back. Who knows where he went or what he's thinking, maybe he just ran off for more doughnuts."

"Okay, then what will you do?" Caroline asked. "I'm not being sidelined, you realize?"

"If I thought you needed to be reined in, Sunshine, I'd keep you with me," Darien said with a smirk. "You need a babysitter."

Greg cracked up. "He's not wrong, kitten."

Caroline just scowled. "You haven't answered my question."

"I'm going to hit the bars like I already planned. Maybe I'll hear something useful about any of this. If someone kidnapped Lucas, then someone else knows," Darien said.

"True. Criminals are worse gossips than grannies at a tea party." Greg chuckled. "I'll try tracking Lucas. If I can get Shakes to tap the cameras around here maybe one of them caught him."

As if on cue, Darien's phone rang.

"Shakes! You're on speaker."

"Well, you want the good news or the bad news?" Shakes didn't bother with niceties.

"Just tell us," Caroline grumbled.

"Hey, C. Your boy left the motel on his own steam. He was talking to someone on the phone, though. He made it to the sidewalk and then halfway down the block before someone stepped out behind him and hit him with something. Looked like a dart maybe. Not elfshot, I can say that much," Shakes said. There was the sound of tapping on a keyboard in the background.

"So he left on his own steam but then was kidnapped?" Spark asked.

"Yep. He staggered a few steps and then went down. The guy that grabbed him made sure to grab his phone, too, so at least there's that. If Lucas can get hold of his phone I'm sure he'll send out an SOS," Shakes said. "Hell, between his basic rogue skills and his magic, I'd be surprised if we don't hear from him soon. Still. I got the plates for the car they shoved him into and unsurprisingly they are not only stolen plates, but they don't belong to the car they're on, which disappears into an underground parking garage with no cameras."

Caroline growled in frustration and Darien once again squeezed her shoulder.

"Get me the location of the garage and I'll head over there," Greg said. "With luck, that's where they're keeping him."

"I somehow doubt it, but I'll send the location to your phone. Good luck." And with that Shakes ended the call. Greg's phone dinged a moment later.

Greg glanced at the screen. "Okay, I–"

"Hey!" A young man who couldn't seem to decide what he wanted to be when he grew up was striding toward them, three more men behind him. They, at least, in their loose jeans and sweatshirts seemed to have settled on "generic thug." Their leader wore a button-up shirt and fitted, dark wash jeans under his hoodie. An Executive Thug, maybe?

Caroline rolled her eyes. This kid–okay, so he was probably older than her by a few years, but he looked almost like he was playing dress-up– was trying to intimidate them. She could tell from his posturing and from the notes of confidence and covetousness in his voice. One syllable told her the whole story.

"Buzz off. We're a bit busy here," she said, turning her back on them before a thought struck her. "Unless you have some information for us. Then we might not put you all on the ground."

Greg grinned and Spark snickered. Darien just stood there, crossing his arms and looking every inch the experienced underworld enforcer that he so often pretended to be. A glance at Darien put a hitch in the kid's stride for a step, but he kept coming. Confident in his buddies' ability to intimidate, no doubt.

"Look, little girl. I'm here to talk to the big boys, and

offer them a deal. Where's the brown one? Robin." The last question was addressed to Darien.

The corner of Darien's eye twitched. "I am going to assume you mean our friend, as his complexion is rather darker than mine due to his mother's genetic heritage. But if you want something, you need to use your manners. Epithets and slurs are not the way to go."

The kid blinked, visibly thrown by the turn in the conversation, but he shrugged it off quick enough.

"*Robin* has gotten his hands on something that used to belong to old man Calder. My employer wants it, and is willing to offer a finders fee for handing it over to us. That's all. We're happy to work out a deal that doesn't involve violence."

Darien glanced at Caroline, who confirmed the truthfulness of the statement.

"What exactly is it that he is supposed to have found?" Darien asked. "The guy winds up with all sorts of things. He's a bit of a magpie."

The kid smirked. "I bet he does. My boss wants the knife. It's an antique and old man Calder picked it up in, shall we say, a less than legal manner, right out from under my boss' nose, then he went and got dead. It's not much, but my boss has his pride. We know Robin took it off the Calder family and are willing to negotiate."

Caroline tried not to growl. This kid was skirting the edge of the truth, hard.

"And why is Lu–Robin more likely to hand it over to you than anyone else?" Darien asked.

"Well, because my friends here are very loyal." He jerked his head back to indicate the muscle behind him. One of the big guys leered at Caroline, another one smirked.

"So?" Greg chimed in. "We've taken down bigger guys."

"Probably not like them." A smug grin crept over the kid's face. "Because none of them are human."

All three men growled now, the sound raising the hairs on the back of Caroline's neck, a reaction to being confronted with a predator. It was a familiar sensation now, and simply served to get her ready for a fight.

Spark grinned at her side. It was just a little bloodthirsty, and the kid's grin shrank a fraction. "Are you? Human, I mean?"

Confidence returned to the kid's expression. "Nope." He held up his palm, the air above it suddenly spinning madly.

"Good. We don't have to feel bad, then," Spark held his own hands up, left palm full of fire. Over his right hand stones and pebbles and dirt flew from their surroundings to swirl madly.

The kid stepped back, eyes wide with surprise. It was, as Mitch had excitedly pointed out at the beginning of their association with the young mage, extremely rare for a magic user to be equally proficient with two elements. Spark was neither pyromagus nor a geomagus. He was both, and they teasingly referred to him as Vulcan's bestie.

Add to that shock Darien's suddenly fang-filled snarl, and Greg's now very toothy grin, and the newcomers were clearly shaken. Still, the goons behind the mage moved, leaving Spark to the kid. That left one shifter for each of them.

"I mean, *I'm* human," Caroline muttered. "You guys aren't *that* cool. I'm cool too."

The one who had leered at Caroline advanced on her and she stepped back a few paces, giving herself some room.

"It's just you and me, sweetie. I'll be happy to make you feel better. There's no shame in giving up, you know. I don't want to hurt you," he said, the leer still firmly in place. "There's much more fun things we could do."

She mentally sighed. "Ugh. You're right about there being no shame in surrendering. So if you want to stand down, I promise I won't think any less of you."

"Oh, sweetie, don't be like that. How about you and me go have some fun when Ace is finished here?" He stepped closer and this time Caroline didn't give up any ground.

"How about no," she said.

"Too bad. We coulda had some fun." He grinned. "I'll try not to be too rough."

When he reached for her she could almost hear Peaches critiquing his moves. The combat instructor would probably critique her defense, as well, but as he always pointed out, any defense is good as long as it works. It took Caroline no time at all to put the overconfident shifter on the ground, his arm twisted up behind his back, rendering it impossible to shift unless he wanted to dislocate his shoulder.

"I don't need to be a paranormal to kick your ass, dude," she grumbled. "I need all the special effects."

She glanced up and saw Greg watching over the prone forms of the other two shifters while Darien came jogging back from their rooms with handcuffs. Spark was sitting on the back of the kid—Ace, she assumed—who was coughing and spitting, even facedown on the pavement.

"I really wish that these guys would stop sending low-rent thugs after us. It's insulting," Caroline said. She was still grumpy about the assumption that she would be easy prey. If it wasn't because she was female, then it was because she wasn't a shifter or a vampire or a mage or whatever. Ugh.

"I'll take low-rent thugs over another kidnapping, thanks," Spark said. "Though I guess I handled that okay."

"I'm not sure I'd say that. Seismologists are still trying to figure out the random volcanic eruption in the Midwest," Darien said, shooting Spark a pointed look. "Okay. Let's get these guys officially arrested and see what we can learn."

18

Caroline stomped back into the motel room, followed somewhat less violently by Spark. He grabbed a bottle of water and then took a seat on the sofa, and she knew he was watching her slam around the room, pulling out some water for herself before setting about making terrible coffee in the tiny, cheap coffee maker the room came with. Greg and Darien had sent her and Spark back to the motel room in case of further developments while the agents took Ace and his friends to the local detention facility.

"They're deliberately sticking me somewhere out of the way to keep me from helping," she growled at Spark, who didn't respond. "I am so sick of being treated like I'm useless. Or worse! Like I'm a liability! Did you see me take down that shifter?"

"I was a bit busy at the time, so no, I didn't," Spark said. "And I think they're trying to teach you patience more than anything else. You can be a bit, how do I put this, more of a leap-before-you-look sort of person."

Caroline growled but didn't respond to the accusation.

"Also, do I need to point out that you're still an intern? That probably makes a difference in the arrest and booking process, and all the paperwork," Spark said, speaking his words slowly and watching her with a bit of concern. "I mean, are you even legally allowed to arrest anyone?"

"That's never made much of a difference before!" she grumbled. He was right, of course. The paperwork was a nightmare when she was involved in the actual arrest. It was bad enough when she was involved in the takedown, but they usually claimed that it was worth the extra form-filling to keep her close enough to watch and evaluate.

She was starting to wonder if they meant babysit.

"Caroline, they're just doing their jobs. We did sort of sneak off to steal things and get involved in some sort of crime-family drama," Spark said.

"And what about looking for Lucas, hmm? Now that they're off booking those morons, who's looking for Lucas? Not us, apparently, because we're stuck here in this stupid motel room!" She grabbed one of the styrofoam cups provided with the cheap coffee and tried unsuccessfully to slam it down. Even the damn inanimate objects were deliberately irritating her.

"Maybe Shakes has found something new? He's had more time to try to track the guys that snatched Lucas. Whoever they were, they didn't leave the dart behind for us to look into, so they're not new at this. They must have some sort of history, right? Maybe Shakes ran their faces through some fancy facial recognition software or something?"

Caroline glared at him for a long moment, letting the powdered creamer dissolve in the coffee.

"That's not a bad idea, I guess," she said, leaving the cup on the desk next to the tiny pot. She sat heavily on the bed and dug her phone from her pocket. "I'm putting him on speaker."

The phone rang once before Shakes's voice rang out. "What, Caroline? I'm trying to figure out where the hell they went."

"Well, I guess that answers that. At least *someone* is looking for him. No idea who those guys were that grabbed him? We figured they weren't amateurs since they took the dart with them."

"No. One of them is a mercenary that I recognized without even searching. He turns up regularly enough that we know his face, but he's a mundane, plain old human merc so he's mostly out of our jurisdiction, and he hasn't been caught yet anyway. If he's involved in working for mages or the paranormal, then he's ours, and since Lucas was the victim and this case's MacGuffin seems to be heavily enchanted, I'd say that's a good bet."

Caroline huffed out a frustrated breath. "You have nothing for us?"

Shakes muttered a bit. "Well, I did learn one fun fact."

"What? What is it?" Caroline sat up and stared at the phone as if Shakes could see her.

"There's a price on Lucas's head, and you and Spark, too," Shakes said. "Although the bounty names him 'Robin' and doesn't name either of you at all, other than as 'known associates.' There's a photo that looks like it was taken in a cafe or something, of you three sitting at a table with a woman I don't recognize. It does say that all three of you have been seen this week in Wilmington."

Caroline frowned.

"Maybe because of Lynn? Someone must have been following her," Spark said, his voice thoughtful.

"She was worried about it. Looks like she had cause to be," Caroline agreed.

"So what has you so worked up, C?" Shakes asked, the clacking of his fingers on the keyboard a constant background to the whole conversation.

"I'm being babysat and I don't need it, dammit," she grumbled.

"We were jumped in the parking lot," Spark cut in. "We took them down easily enough, but the guys told us to wait here while they took the attackers to get booked. Caroline is a bit put out at the inactivity."

"I don't need to be babysat! I don't need to be carefully kept out of the way and protected while the so-called big boys do things!" Caroline protested. "I'm perfectly capable!"

"Nobody thinks you're incapable, C, but we do think you're inexperienced, young, and despite how Point assigns cases, you are still an intern. Sometimes that does make a difference," Shakes said.

"Careful, man. I tried to point that out already," Spark said. "It's a sore spot."

Caroline ground her teeth together and screamed through them. "So what? The fact remains that I am *not* useless, and making me sit here where I might as well be a princess in a damn tower is a waste of everyone's time! When do we go find Lucas? He didn't sleep for *days* when we were looking for Greg! Why aren't we looking for him just as hard?"

"I *am* looking, Caroline," Shakes sighed. The clacking of his keyboard stopped and there was a rustling noise. "Look, I haven't managed to trace these guys yet. They were very clever in where they parked and if they changed vehicles or went into the building or somewhere else, I just don't know. I'm tracking the three cars that have left the structure in the last half hour and so far I found one very tired-looking housewife going to the grocery store, and another woman heading out on a date or something. This third guy is still driving and looks to be headed out of state, so I doubt he's our guy if they want the dagger that you are currently guarding."

Spark nodded at everything Shakes said. "Also, Darien and Greg intend to go on to do what they planned to before Ace and his lackeys decided to do stupid things and get arrested. They just need to finish booking them and making sure they're secure before either of them can head out. If there's a rumor to be heard at a bar, D will hear it, and Greg is an excellent tracker, you know that."

It still felt unreasonable to Caroline, but she couldn't argue with anything wither of them said. It was faster to ignore the whole thing for now. She had bigger problems to focus on than her own feelings.

"So, how much are we worth?" she finally asked.

"Twenty grand for you and Spark, seventy-five for Lucas. It's an open contract. And even though I don't see any sign that anyone's taken it, it's possible that someone snatched Lucas in the hopes of a payday. I've watched the video several times now and it was a very workmanlike snatch, so I think we can confirm that they were professionals."

Caroline snorted. "Unlike the thugs who tried to intimidate us in the parking lot."

"Apparently. You seem to have all the luck, Caroline," Shakes said. "Anyhow, it's probably best if you and Spark stay out of sight for a bit."

Caroline glared at the phone sitting on the bed. "Did Darien put you up to this?"

"C, you can *hear* I'm not lying to you," Shakes groaned. "And you know perfectly well I'm on Team No More Kidnappings. How many times have you been snatched now? Three times?"

"I don't think the first time counts. I was in high school and didn't know anything about you guys," she grumbled. She could understand his position, but like hell was she going to give him any support in keeping her hidden away. So what if maybe she got herself into a few scrapes? They all turned out okay in the end! "I'm not letting you guys stick me in the tower to stay safe."

"Calm yourself, conclusion-jumper. You do what you want. Just try not to get kidnapped or killed, okay? That's really all I'm asking."

"Um, me too," Spark cut in. "I also do not want to get kidnapped for someone's next paycheck."

"It's not like I ever *want* to get held captive. And thank you very much, but why aren't you lecturing Greg? Mr. I-won't-listen-to-advice got himself captured by doing specifically what *I* told him not to do!" She was never going to let him live that down.

"Probably because he wasn't involved in any cases at the time. Nothing major, anyway, and there was no reasonable expectation that he would be put in danger," Shakes pointed out.

"Um, except everything that felt super hinky about it? Even *I* thought it felt hinky," she replied. "At least we got Spark out of the whole mess."

"Gee, thanks. I feel the love." He rolled his eyes. "Okay, Shakes. Thanks for the heads-up on the bounty. Caroline, can you at least promise to take it seriously and make a plan before you charge off to do something?"

"I don't just *charge off*." Did they have to be so damn sensible? "I don't understand how you guys can be so calm when Lucas is missing."

"Like we said, we're already doing everything we can to find him, already. If you can think of another angle to tackle, then great," Shakes said. "I can't track Lucas's phone and I can't get into it to check the call logs, but I do have a request in to the phone company to get the logs the old-fashioned way. If that call he was on was from anything other than a burner then we'll be another step further."

"I hate waiting." Caroline flopped back onto the bed.

"But you're so good at it." Shakes couldn't finish his sentence with a straight face, as evidenced by the laughter in the last few words.

"Look, you."

"I'll call you the second I hear something, okay? I promise C. Keep Spark safe, okay? Try not to get kidnapped yourself. All that stuff. Now let me do my job," Shakes said, still obviously amused.

"Fine," she huffed.

"Bye, Shakes. Thanks." Spark reached over to pick up the phone.

"No problem. Later." The line went dead.

"Sorry it wasn't better news," Spark said, handing her phone over.

"Is it ever?" she asked. "Hey, didn't I make coffee?"

"I think it's cold, coffee-themed sludge by now," Spark answered.

Caroline sighed. It was going to be a long afternoon.

19

"Oh, that's an easy one. What is Washington DC?" Caroline grumbled at the television. Spark rolled his eyes and smirked as one of the contestants buzzed in with the same answer.

"I didn't know some French dude designed DC," he said. "Learn something new every day I guess."

"Yeah. It was one of the few random things that I actually remember from high school history. Pierre L'Enfant was a real pain in the butt, though, if I remember right." Caroline dug another cashew out of the carton in front of her and popped it into her mouth. "I'm getting a lot better with chopsticks."

"Darien's favorite stakeout food, huh?" Spark grinned.

It was dark outside the window now, and they were slowly making their way through the Chinese food spread out on the coffee table. Darien and Greg had both checked in over the long afternoon, Darien telling them the list of bars he planned to visit and Greg with the news of no news when he got to the parking garage. The vehicle Shakes identified as the one belonging to the mercenaries had been wiped clean with bleach for good measure, so not even Greg's excellent nose could follow them.

"Mine, actually," she said. "It's easy to just pick at it over an hour or two while we watch whatever it is we're watching, and it's also pretty easy to close up quick if we need to move fast, but it's also pretty dang tasty."

Spark tipped his head and nodded slowly. "Yeah, okay. I can see that." He was about to add something when his phone rang. "Oh, hey Greg, any news?Huh. Hang on, I'm putting you on speaker or Caroline will smother me in my sleep tonight."

Greg's laugh rang out when Spark thumbed the button.

"We can't have that. I'm pretty sure she'd lose her job if she committed murder," Greg chuckled.

"Jerks, both of you," she grumbled.

"Hey, kitten. I'm sorry to report that I have had no more luck than Shakes on tracking these jerks from the garage. It's like they disappeared into thin air. They definitely took precautions against paranormals, though. The bleach burned my nose out for an hour."

Caroline scrunched up her face. "I'm sorry. That stuff's bad enough for a human nose. I can't imagine what it's like for you."

"Not a lot of fun, I'll tell you that much," he answered. "The good news is that I did pick up a scrap of Lucas's scent in the far corner of the garage. I suspect that they carried him over and brushed against the wall without noticing. The bad news is that means they got in another vehicle since there's no doors or anything over there. I already called it in to Shakes, so he's going back over the footage again."

"Are there no other exits from the place? Like, on other levels or something?" Spark asked.

"I haven't seen any, but then I didn't search too hard

when I first got here. I was going on the assumption that I could pick up something useful from the getaway vehicle. I'm about to go over the whole place again, to make sure I didn't miss anything. Have you heard from Darien yet?"

Caroline sighed.

"I'll take that as a no, then?" Greg sounded way too amused.

"Nothing useful. Just that the first place was nearly empty, so he was going to head out to his second stop. He's probably there by now," Spark said. He shot a glare at Caroline but she was already stewing. Even when they had been searching for Greg she hadn't felt this useless.

"There has to be *something*," she said. "We have to find him."

"We will, Caroline." Greg's voice was serious now. "I'm not going to give up, even if I strike out here. If I can't get anything from here, then I'll head over to meet D and come up with a new plan."

Caroline's phone beeped with an incoming text message. "Maybe that's him now, hang on."

She pulled out her phone and her heart stopped. It wasn't a text from Darien, it was a photo, sent from Lucas's phone. In it, he lay on a light blue carpet, bound hand and foot, new bruises blooming over his face and a smear of blood on his shirt. His eyes were closed, and for a heart-stopping moment, Caroline thought he was dead.

"Oh, shit." Spark peered over Caroline's shoulder.

"What is it, Spark?"

"It's a photo of Lucas and he doesn't look good. And I have some decent points of reference for not-good, Greg, " Spark answered. "I'll get Caroline to forward it to you guys."

"There's a message, too," she murmured. Glancing down at the text she read it out loud. "You three have had plenty of time to recover the dagger. Bring it to us or Robin won't make it past dawn." Following that was a photo of her and Lucas in the car outside the diner they picked up breakfast from a few days ago.

The silence that reached through the phone made Caroline shiver.

"I assume they also included directions for where to go?" Greg asked after a long moment. His voice was calm in a way that spoke volumes about how angry he was.

"Yeah. Come alone, go to this place, all that sort of thing," she said. "I'm going to ask for proof that he's alive. This photo...it's bad, Greg. He needs a hospital."

"I'll let people know to expect him soon," Greg answered. "Caroline—"

"Yeah?" She paused in her typing to glance at the phone and became aware of Spark watching her carefully through narrowed eyes. "What?"

"Don't do it," Spark said.

"Do what?"

"You know damn well what he means, kitten," Greg growled. "Don't go scurrying off on your own in some half-baked attempt to rescue Lucas. Let us do our job. Have Shakes trace the text. He can't get to it from Lucas's phone, but maybe he can do it from yours. And he can check out wherever it is that you're supposed to deliver this dagger to."

"Good idea." Spark nodded.

"Shit," Caroline muttered. "Well, he's breathing, guys, but that's about all I can say. They sent a ten-second video of him breathing, with someone's tablet next to his face. The time shown is just a couple of minutes ago."

"Okay, so that's a positive. He's alive," said Greg.

"And they don't know what he can do with a tablet, even if his hands are bound behind his back." Spark smirked. "When he wakes up, I'd bet it's only a few minutes before he sends out alerts via every phone in his range."

"True enough," Greg agreed. "Okay, I'm going to go meet up with D. Caroline, you get that information to Shakes right away. Spark...try to keep her out of trouble. D and I will be back soon."

"I'm perfectly capable, thank you," Caroline huffed.

"You have a lot of skills, Caroline, and you're excellent in a pinch, but you are also not a full agent and you're a bit impulsive," Greg said. "I promise we aren't going to exclude you from the rescue. All I ask is that you don't run off on your own. Wait for us to get there. Let us do our homework on the whole thing and come up with some sort of plan. Okay?"

"Fine," she huffed. Greg was right, but she didn't have to like it. "I'm calling Shakes. Go get Darien and get your butts back here so we can go rescue Lucas."

The room fell into silence as she texted Shakes, who took the time to swear creatively via text message and then stopped responding entirely, so presumably, he was working on tracking down anything he could.

"There's not even any way we can identify his location from the video or the picture," she said. She knew she was whining, but dammit, they felt so close now. "It's just a plain blue carpet, and the only sound in the background is his breathing, which doesn't sound great. He needs a doctor."

"Yeah. I'm honestly worried, C." Spark grimaced. "But you can't go haring off and following their directions. You understand that, right?"

She huffed, the frustration mounting again. "I know. Doesn't mean I have to like it"

Spark shimmied over and nudged her shoulder with his

own. "We're going to save Lucas, but not at the cost of you."

Caroline groaned. "I get it, already! Stop trying to convince me!"

"Okay, okay," Spark chuckled. "I'll trust you."

They sat in silence for a long moment, Caroline staring at the cartons of Chinese food still sitting on the table in front of them.

"I wish there was more we could do," Spark sighed. "I suppose if we narrow locations down a bit, then I could go see if the ground holds any traces of his magic. It's not a super reliable skill yet, but it can't hurt to try. I just need a smaller search radius than 'all of Wilmington.'"

Caroline grimaced and patted his knee. "At least you have a skill that is useful at all right now. All I have is determination and human stubbornness." She glared around the room feeling even more stuck. Her gaze landed on Lucas's computer.

"I mean, we were planning on just taking the thing back to Mitch and Ollie, right? Why didn't we just leave when he got the sheath?" she wondered out loud.

"Good question. I think we all got sidetracked with the idea of figuring out why Calder wants it so badly and we kind of forgot to just make our own lives easier." Spark shrugged.

Caroline huffed and nodded. "Yeah, it's easy to get swept up in the mystery of it all and forget that it's not our job to wrap everything up in a pretty bow like an Agatha Christie novel." She stood up. "And honestly, Lucas wasn't exactly agitating for us to get out of Dodge. Think he was up to something?"

"Well, if he was, I don't think it was particularly nefarious," Spark said. He sat up and started closing the food containers. "He's not a bad guy, just a bit shady. I think he's got massive trust issues."

Caroline snorted at that. "You think?" She stood and wandered over to where Lucas's computer and tablet were still sitting on the table and peered down at them. "Still. He left his tools here for any of us to poke at. I mean, sure, he's probably got them protected, but this tablet is basically his magic wand. I don't think I've ever seen him without it, unless it's in his bag which is strapped to him."

She ran her finger along the edge of it.

"It's kind of funny, too," Spark said. "You'd think he'd keep replacing it, getting the newest version or the latest, fastest, whatever. That one's at least five years old."

"I bet it runs better than any of the new ones, too," Caroline said. She sat in the chair that was still pulled out slightly, and swiveled to face the keyboard. She ran her finger lightly over the keys and startled when the screen lit up. "Oops. Didn't mean to actually wake the thing."

The computer's tiny camera light lit up and Caroline's face appeared on the screen. A second later the words "Welcome Caroline" flashed under her startled image, then the screen cleared and Lucas's desktop screen sat there, waiting for her to...what?

"Um." She turned to Spark, wide-eyed. "Maybe he doesn't have such serious trust issues after all?"

Spark peered over her shoulder, blinking slowly. "The question now, I guess, is can we use this to find Lucas, and if we can, how?"

"I don't know yet, but we'd better figure it out fast," Caroline said. She took a deep breath then put her fingers to the keys. "I have a bad feeling that Lucas doesn't have a ton of time."

20

Once she got over her shock, Caroline was confronted with a single icon in the middle of the screen, a file folder titled "For Caroline – Read Me."

With few other options, she followed the directions and opened the file. A text document popped open to fill the screen.

Caroline,

If you're reading this, things have gone terribly wrong somehow, and I'm in trouble. Shocking, I know. But this is us, after all, and no plan is going to go exactly the way we want. When you close this document, you'll find all the relevant information, I hope, and if I don't come back in a few days, the rest of everything will unlock. I've set up several spells that will help you access everything at that point, both here and back at my house. Do whatever makes sense with it all.

If the choice comes down to saving me or saving the world, you know what to do, but I can honestly tell you that I have complete faith that you and the guys will find some way to pull me out of the fire. Just try not to get kidnapped or killed in the process, okay?

Lucas

Well, damn.

"If that's not one hell of a vote of confidence, I don't know what is," Spark said softly, just over her shoulder.

"Yeah." Caroline felt like she was choking on the word and her eyes stung. Spark wrapped his arms around her and squeezed her in a tight hug until she sniffled and reached up to pat his wrist.

"Thanks. I'm okay now," she said. She knew her voice still sounded a bit wobbly, but she was determined to see what Lucas had turned up. "Now then, let's see what he's got here."

She closed the text file and was startled to see several folders neatly labeled "Dagger," "Junior," "Senior," and "??"

"Guess we start at the beginning," she muttered.

"Sure, but where's it all begin?" Spark asked, standing up and glaring at the files.

"Well, the dagger is the oldest thing in this situation, so let's start there," she said, and clicked on the file.

Two hours later she had learned a lot more about medieval weaponry than she had ever thought she would, and found that Lucas could trace this very dagger back at least to the middle of the ninteenth century. Apparently, in 1843 a businessman in London was in possession of this thing, and Lucas found an actual portrait of the man with his hand on the dagger and what looked like maybe a ledger sitting on the table next to him The photo was taken in 1857, and Caroline was both impressed that Lucas could find the photo to identify the dagger—which was clearly visible and easy to compare with the one in their possession—and that the picture from so long ago was so clear. The man claimed that much of his success was due to his keen eye for a good bargain, and to the dagger.

"Hey, Spark," she called. He had retreated to the bed to work through some exercises Mitch had given him to help his magic control. "Come check this out!" she called. "Oh! I think there are printed copies of these photos. Look in his laptop bag, would you?"

Spark shook his hands out and extinguished the lick of flame he had been dancing around the bedspread before standing up and coming over to dig through the satchel Lucas used.

"God, he's a bit of a packrat," Spark said, amused. He slid a file folder onto the table behind the laptop. "Here's a bunch of pictures, but there's a ton of stuff in here. Oh hell!"

"What? Stop rummaging through his stuff." Caroline sat back.

"Check this out, though," Spark said. He pulled something out from the bottom of the bag and put it in front of her with a thunk.

Caroline blinked down at the dagger in front of her. "Is that...Didn't Greg wrap that thing up and stick it somewhere?"

Spark grinned. "He did. Well, he wrapped up the one that Lucas brought back from the pirate's treasure chest. This one's not enchanted. I can't sense any magic on it at all, and the one that he stashed at the museum was very clearly covered in a spell. I think this is a fake that he was going to hand over if the Calders insisted. I can't sense even a hint of magic on this thing."

Caroline blinked at the dagger in front of her. If Spark wasn't assuring her of the difference, she would never have known. He rose, went over to the closet and dug around for a moment before coming back to the table, the sheathed dagger in one hand and the wrapping cloth in the other. He dropped the cloth, pulled the dagger free, and placed it beside the fake.

"Damn, that's really close," Spark said. "The colors are a bit off, but really not too bad."

"Yeah. I don't remember him working on this. Do you think that maybe he planned to swap the thing out in the first place?" Caroline frowned at the pair of weapons. She shivered. "Either way, put that sheath away, would you? It gives me the creeps. And look at that photo."

Spark did as she asked, securing the real dagger away again and sitting on the sofa with the file folder.

"So this businessman claimed, several times, that his success was related to owning that dagger. He says in a letter to his friend that it helped him 'cut through the serpentine words of those who would abuse my good nature.' Whatever that means." She wrinkled her nose at the screen.

"Think he straight-up threatened to cut them?" Spark asked with a grin.

"Well, that would certainly get his *point* across, wouldn't you say?"

Spark laughed. "Nice."

"Anyhow, after he died, it was passed along to his daughter who sold the business and a lot of her father's things before heading off on adventures unknown. The dagger got sold to a business partner who claimed it was both an excellent tool for business and a sentimental reminder of his friend," Caroline continued.

"So whatever the enchantment is, it's not used as a weapon in a conventional sense, it sounds like." Spark leaned back on the sofa. "I wonder what it is?"

Caroline shook her head. "Everyone just sort of talks around it."

"Well, that's not very helpful," Spark groaned. "What happened after that?"

Caroline's answer was stopped by the whir of the door's lock opening. The sound of rain and the smell of wet pavement blew in as the door cracked, preceding Greg who limped in, all but carrying Darien, who sagged against Greg's side, one arm wrapped over the bigger man's shoulders. Once the door closed behind them, the sound of the latch clicking into place almost loud in the sudden quiet, Darien let his head fall against Greg's body and seemed to give up all effort now that he knew he was safe.

"Shit!" Spark jumped up and was under Darien's other arm and supporting him in seconds. "Darien gets the bed and you're on the sofa, big guy. What happened?"

They gently lowered Darien onto the mattress and Caroline took over, pulling off his shoes and settling his feet carefully on the bed. He groaned and muttered, but he didn't rouse.

"Got jumped outside of the last bar. The place was so damn loud my ears were ringing, so we didn't hear them come up behind us."

Greg eased himself onto the sofa and grunted. Spark dashed into the other room and came back with a first aid kit.

"You know the drill by now. Off with the shirt," Spark ordered, and Greg groaned again, but did as he was told. A purple bruise wrapped over his left bicep and there were a few scratches that looked like they were made by claws. "So, you got jumped. What happened that took out our badass vamp?"

Caroline wanted to know the same thing. The first time she ever met the man, in a damp cellar room being used as a prison, he had looked very similar. And that was after being hit with several elfshot darts and being beaten extensively. She grabbed the cloth Spark handed her and started wiping away the trail of blood that caked his jaw, searching for the injury it came from.

"There were about six hundred of them, seemed like," Greg said. He hissed when Spark dabbed an alcohol swab over one particularly long scratch. "I think it started as an attempt on us specifically, then ended up spilling into the bar where it became more of a free-for-all. They pulled out the smashed bar stools and broken beer bottles and so on, all the classics, and then someone got their hands on a damned pipe. Smashed D hard on the shoulder, which knocked him off balance enough that they could pile on and take him down. He was wading through them easily enough before that."

"God," Spark muttered, and dug into the first aid kit for another bandage. "That's the last one. You're not too badly off, overall, but I don't like that bruise."

"Yeah. They tried to get me with the damn pipe too. They were rather upset when I took it from them and threw it over the damn bar."

Spark chuckled. "Bet that gave them a moment to think better of their life choices."

"Yeah." Greg rolled his head back and forth, and stretched. Spark handed him a bottle of water and he gulped it down.

"Why isn't he waking up?" Spark asked. "I thought vampires were famously hard to keep down?"

Greg grimaced, but Caroline was the one who answered. "They are, but they can still get the shit kicked out of them. He's had more than a couple of bad injuries since I've known him. Where's his kit?" She looked over at Greg who gazed over her shoulder in thought.

"I think it's in the closet in the other room. Spark, would you grab it?"

Spark was already halfway through the door before Greg finished speaking. A moment later he returned, the small black duffel already open as he dug through it.

"They're cans, right? Like soda cans of blood?" he asked.

"Yeah. They look like more tomato juice than anyone would want to drink in one go. Jumbo soda can sized," Caroline answered.

Spark frowned and set the bag on the table. "When was the last time he looked in here?" He started taking things out and placing them neatly next to the bag. "It's sort of a giant mess. I'm not seeing any cans."

"He had it under his desk when we left, so it couldn't have been long," Greg answered. "Oh hell."

"Shit," Caroline groaned. "It was under his desk? That's where he chucks it when he needs to repack it all. I bet he needed to restock and hadn't gotten to it. You didn't think to check?"

"I was distracted with all the being annoyed at you I was doing," Greg grumbled.

"There's some more first aid in here though, and some spare clothes," Spark said, as if that would make up for the missing blood packs.

"Guess we'll just have to wait it out." Greg sighed. "I'm going to bed. We'll both be fine in the morning, and we can yell at him for not doing a better job of keeping his go bag actually ready to go."

"I keep telling him to do it right away after he gets back from using it, but does he listen to me?" Caroline muttered. She took a pocketknife from the neatly laid out contents of the bag and flicked it open. "He'll need the damn spare clothes," she said just before cutting the bloody T-shirt off him to reveal more injuries. "I'm going to kick his damn ass when he wakes up."

"Let's leave her to it," Greg said, reaching out to tug on Spark's sleeve. "Best not to get in her way when she's in this mood."

Caroline heard them leave the room and kept cleaning up her partner, who grumbled a few times when she swiped over a particularly bad bruise with some torn skin right where the impact must have been.

"That looks like it was steel-toed-boots," she said. "Jerks. If you were awake, I could at least feed you, you inconsiderate numbskull. It's too damned dangerous to feed an unconscious vamp, dammit. I do not need another lecture on paranormal first aid safety." She went over the mental list of first aid she *could* do for him, and did her best to follow it, but Darien stayed stubbornly unconscious.

She was just debating the merits of dribbling some blood into a glass and feeding him that way when her phone beeped. She pulled it out and almost threw up at the short, looped video of a man, easily as big as Greg, try to drive what looked like half a stop sign post into Darien's skull, only missing because Darien moved to block a punch from someone else. Darien stumbled and went down almost immediately to the pavement and was surrounded by bodies so the camera could no longer see him.

Eleven seconds of fight footage. Then a message: *Time's ticking, and Robin here isn't the only one we're watching. Now, let's see if you can follow instructions.*

Dammit.

21

Caroline took a steadying breath and squeezed the bag in her lap before she opened the door of the car.

"Hey, you okay?" the driver asked, genuine concern lacing his voice.

"Yeah. Just nervous." She dug up a smile for him. "Getting summoned by the family is rarely a good thing, you know?"

The guy chuckled. "No kidding. Good luck!"

"Thanks." She got out and closed the door gently before waving him off. It was nice to come across decent people, and he was right to be worried for her, after all. She hadn't even lied. She was heading to meet family, just not *her* family. If she was right and this was Calder pulling the strings, then she was taking the whole damn bunch of them down. The only person that they hadn't gotten their hands on now was Spark, and Caroline wasn't about to let that happen.

She stepped up to the front door of the lavish beach house and rang the bell as directed. It was a nice place, she had to admit. A nice change from the usual dirty back alley or half-abandoned warehouse she was used to confronting bad guys in. She had a moment to reflect that fancy doesn't always mean easy, though, so best to be on guard. With that thought, she rang the bell.

It wasn't more than a second before the door opened and the most disreputable-looking butler she had ever met glared at her.

"I have an appointment," she said with as much aloof unconcern as she could muster. It actually got an amused smirk out of the guy, so she counted it as a win.

He turned and led her down a hallway and into a lavishly decorated room, all done up beachy creams and taupes and blues.

"Have a seat. I'll tell the boss you're here." With that pronouncement, he turned and left.

Caroline assumed there were cameras everywhere and she was being watched closely, so she simply sat and waited, her bag on her knees. It didn't take more than a few minutes before a slim, oily woman crept into the room. Caroline eyed her as she stepped over to stand next to the chair Caroline currently sat in, her skirt swirling around her ankles and a hooded sweatshirt at least three sizes too big making her look even scrawnier than she must have been under all that fabric.

There was no way this woman was in shape enough, physically, to be a bodyguard. Caroline herself was fairly slim, but she still had muscle from all her training, and the newcomer had almost no muscle tone whatsoever. In fact, she looked more like she was in need of a shower and a few solid meals. This must be a mage, then. Maybe to verify the dagger? Perhaps to try to control Caroline herself, since she had easily taken down several of the previous goons sent after her. Perhaps this was the earth mage that was watching the area around Calder's mansion?

Well, that would complicate things just a bit.

"Welcome, Miss Sunshine!"

Caroline turned from eyeing the mage to blink at Jeff Calder Junior. It was too bad he was a criminal jackass, Caroline thought idly. With his red-blond hair styled to look carelessly rumpled and his tailored suit jacket hanging open to reveal the artfully unbuttoned shirt, he could easily be a model striding into a photoshoot. Especially when he sent her a charming smile. The jerk was alarmingly good-looking.

"Calder."

"Oh please, call me Jeff. I know it's an old joke, but everyone *did* insist on calling my father *Mr. Calder*. Makes me feel like I should look around the room for the old man when anyone calls me that," he said. He took a seat on the sofa across the low coffee table from her and propped his ankle upon his other knee, leaning back casually. "I'm sorry for the lateness of the meeting, but we're all so busy it seems. Arranging it seemed almost impossible for a bit."

"Funny thing about that, isn't it?" Caroline said with a smile. "So, Robin is usually in charge of these things, so I'm sure you can understand how his absence has made everything rather difficult."

"Indeed," Calder said. "Sudden changes in leadership are so difficult to navigate. When my father passed away it threw everything into chaos, it felt like. I'm still trying to gather up all the reins of his business."

Caroline nodded. "Your mother dying so suddenly, so soon after was no doubt even more chaotic."

His smile turned slightly wolfish. "Such a tragedy, that accident."

The man was damned slick, and he didn't feel even the

slightest remorse for either of his parents' deaths, both of which he orchestrated. Almost like he was broadcasting on purpose, his voice was telling her all sorts of things that were good to know, even if she couldn't submit them as evidence, but none of it was what she was after. Caroline needed to get him to at least think about where Lucas was. Remembering to call him by his alias wasn't helping her concentrate, either. "At least Robin isn't dead."

"No, that is true," he admitted. "But life moves so fast. Things change on a dime at any moment."

Caroline grinned. Got him. Damn, Lucas was close, but she would have to play this carefully.

"So, down to business, then," she said. "Before things take another turn."

Calder sat up and clapped his hands together before rubbing them like a villain in a melodrama. "Wonderful! Best to get business out of the way, indeed. Have you got it?"

"Yeah." Caroline stood and dug in her bag before she turned and dropped it on the seat of the chair. As she turned back, she banged right into the mage, who was leaning closer with a sullen glare. Caroline had to put a hand on the woman just to keep them both from falling to the floor in a heap.

"Excuse me, manners much?" Caroline growled at the woman, who straightened again, but didn't change her expression.

Putting the woman out of her mind for the moment, she gripped the wrapping cloth tighter as she turned back to Calder. "How do I know that you won't just have us both killed as soon as I hand this over? What sort of guarantee can you give me? Right now I have a weapon, at least."

"I'm afraid you'll just have to trust me, Miss Sunshine,"

he said before sweeping his arm around the room. "But look. I have come to meet with you with no bodyguards other than Rachel there, and I have to admit. I've seen some video of you in action. I doubt she could even land a punch against you."

Caroline flicked a glance at Rachel, who was scowling at Calder now. Caroline bit back a smirk, then turned back and put the bundle on the table. "Now where's Lu—Robin? He looked like he needs a doctor, and I want to get him there ASAP."

Calder wasn't listening to her. He pounced on the wrapped dagger and tore the cloth away from the blade, which gleamed baleful and deadly in the room's lighting. He laughed, delighted as the wrapper fluttered to the table and he gripped the hilt firmly. "At last! Nobody can dispute that I control this family."

"That *we* do, you mean?" a woman's voice corrected him firmly from just outside the door.

"Of course! Come in, darling, come in!" Calder crowed. His eyes glittered, but never strayed from the blade. Caroline didn't want to look at the woman who glided in, her expensive heels silent on the lush carpet. This actually stung. This...this was the unexpected twist that Caroline might not get over.

"I'm glad to see that you're more useful than Robin is, Miss Sunshine," Lynn said with a triumphant purr. "That boy was easy enough to yank around, but honestly. He simply wasn't pulling his weight the way we needed him to."

"Lynn. Wow. I did not see this coming, and it's tough to bullshit me," Caroline said. "I mean, we knew that one of Jeffy's cousins was into the whole family business thing, but I honestly believed you, which is legitimately impressive. I didn't *trust* you, granted, but I did believe you. I frankly can't remember the last time I couldn't detect bullshit when it was being shoveled at me that hard."

Lynn laughed, the sound bright and cheerful. "Oh, Sunshine. With as much practice as I've had talking my way around that thing, fooling one ordinary human was easy as pie."

"Okay, first: you don't get to call me that so please stop," Caroline growled. She was going to have to smack Lucas for his terrible planning. She'd have been fine with more Robin Hood–themed names even if it meant she would be Maid Marion, but "Sunshine" was reserved. "Second: explain. You talked around a *letter opener?*"

Lynn blinked at her in surprise, then laughed again. Calder grinned as well and held a hand out to his cousin, who took it and settled into his side. Settled in far too close for Caroline's comfort.

"Wait a second. Oh, ew, are you *together?* Man, just when I thought this case couldn't get ickier," she said. "You're *cousins.*"

Calder cleared his throat and Rachel ran her hand down his arm.

"*Technically*, we are only related by law. Her father married my father's sister long after we were both born. We are step-cousins, I suppose you could say," Calder said, sending Lynn a besotted smile. "Not that it matters. You and Robin will be dead soon, and Lynn and I can start expanding. Albert!"

He called out the last word and the door opened almost instantly and the butler goon stepped inside.

"Yeah?"

"Miss whatever-she-wants-to-be-called is done here. Take her to Robin then dispose of them both," Lynn said. She wasn't even looking at Caroline anymore, having dismissed her as young and human and female. Calder at least was watching her steadily.

"Rachel, go with him, and if she gives either of you any trouble, flatten her," he said. "Maybe call some of the other men, as well."

"Honestly, she's just one girl," Lynn chided him.

"Yes, love, but I've seen the videos of her taking men down who were twice her size. I'm not going to underestimate her," he answered. It was maybe the first genuinely intelligent thing Caroline had heard him say.

"I suppose." She shrugged one elegant shoulder.

"Can you at least tell me what that thing's supposed to do, before you have me hauled off and murdered?" Caroline asked. The hair on the back of her neck started to stand on end, and her skin itched with awareness. She tried to keep the grin off her face.

"I suppose it won't hurt." Lynn shrugged again. "This blade slices through lies. It will reveal to whoever holds it what the truth is, regardless of what the speaker says."

She smiled, an expression almost as sharp as the blade she stroked. "You haven't uttered one falsehood since you handed this over. We would have felt the lie tingle through our fingers as the dagger reacted."

Caroline's mouth dropped open, trying to say something, anything really, but not finding the words she settled on laughing. Pretty soon she was bent over, hands on her knees, and gasping for breath. "Oh, oh god."

"She gonna be okay?" Albert rumbled.

"She'll be dead soon, so it hardly matters," Calder answered. "But not before she explains all this. What is so damned funny?"

"Oh, oh man. Where to start," Caroline gasped as she caught her breath. "Okay, first things first, I guess. I don't *need* a magic knife to pick up on bullshit. That's why it's so hard to lie to me, lady. I can pick up on lies just from someone grunting, which is why my coworkers keep pulling me into their meetings and interrogations. Whatever it is you learned to get around that skill is seriously impressive."

"Coworkers?" Calder started to ask, but Lynn cut him off.

"What do you mean you don't need a spell? Maybe we are too hasty to order your death," she said, leaning forward.

Caroline got the impression that Lynn was about to try joining the Kidnap Caroline Club. Caroline could only grin.

"I mean I have an empath somewhere in my family tree and they passed along some presents," she said. From the hallway the sound of the front door crashing open sounded clear as day making everyone but Caroline jump. "And yes, my coworkers. If you'd really done your homework, Jeffy, you'd know who they are already, but please allow me to make formal introductions. I believe that is my partner, Special Agent Darien Webb, Federal Paranormal Activities Agency on his way in." Caroline smirked and gestured to the door just as it slammed open to reveal a very angry vampire.

22

The moment of stunned silence didn't last long. Calder roared for more security and Albert swung into action, fur sprouting along his arms as he took a battle-ready half form. Caroline took a moment to be impressed—not a lot of shifters bothered perfecting the skill, not even those who were trained warriors. Greg told her it was a pain in the butt to learn and tough to hold on to, so the fact that Albert was not only able to hold it but seemed to prefer to fight in that form was worth the moment of attention.

Darien seemed to agree since he focused on Albert immediately.

Rachel growled and flung her hands out, jarring slightly when nothing happened.

"Let me help you," Caroline said. She turned slightly and grabbed the woman's wrist, pulling it smoothly toward herself to tug Rachel off balance. The mage flailed to try to stay upright, but it only took Caroline a few seconds to put the woman on the ground and yank her too-long sleeves over her hands. Using the ends, she wrapped the mage up tightly and tied the cuffs of the sweatshirt together behind her.

"There. Nice and snug and safely out of the way," Caroline said to the snarling, swearing woman. "You sit tight, we'll get you appropriately cuffed in a minute."

"Who the hell do you think you are?" Lynn roared. She shoved Calder at Caroline as she herself backed up behind the sofa and edged toward the door. Caroline noted that she kept the dagger clutched to her chest.

"I *think* I'm Caroline Peters, FPAA Agent in training, and you really don't need that thing anymore. It's not the one you wanted anyway." Caroline ducked the punch that Calder optimistically threw at her, and put him down as fast as she had the mage. Behind her, she heard Albert grunt and then a thud that told her he, too, was on the ground. The sharp snap of the FPAA's special handcuffs echoed through the room.

"Now then, Miss whoever-you-are," Darien growled, his words softened by speaking around his fangs. "If you're very smart you're going to come quietly. You're outclassed."

"Hah!" Rachel shouted triumphantly from behind Caroline. She spun to see the mage had worked one of her arms out of the sleeve wrapped around her torso in the best-improvised straight-jacket Caroline could manage, and she was now stretching out the neck of the garment to free it completely. "I'm going to *kill you* for this! You absolute bitch!"

She launched herself at Caroline, her fingers stretched out and her lips moving through some sort of spell. Darien snarled and lurched into motion. Caroline stood patiently as he tackled the mage to the ground, and hissed into her face.

Rachel screamed, then started panicking. "Don't let him eat me! Please! Oh god oh god ohgodohgodohgod!"

"Oh for the love of... You have the right to remain silent, lady, *please* use it," Darien growled. He pulled another pair of suppressor cuffs from another pocket and wrestled Rachel's arms free enough to put them on her. He easily lifted her from the floor and deposited her on the sofa in as much comfort as she could get, then turned to pull plastic cuffs out and address the wannabe mob boss still on the floor.

"Man, tactical pants are so handy. I didn't realize you brought assault gear," Caroline commented mildly as Darien zip-tied Calder and put him next to Rachel on the sofa. "But where's your helmet?"

"I didn't pack all of it, since I was only here to babysit. I only had what was in my trunk," he answered, shooting her a fierce glare with his still-crimson eyes. "And we are going to be talking about this later, C."

She just smirked and turned back to Lynn who was now jabbing at a button on the wall.

"Well, hell. I think she just called the cavalry. You bring Greg and Spark?" Caroline asked. A door somewhere slammed and the whole room shook violently, making Rachel squeak in alarm. "I guess you did."

"I hope Spark doesn't bring the whole damn building down on us," Darien said.

"No kidding. This beach mansion nonsense can't be as structurally sound as that underground bunker slash villain's lair thing Aldebrand had going on," Caroline agreed. "He almost brought that place down on us. But then he was pretty pissed, what with the way those jerks were threatening Greg."

She turned to Lynn. "Is that something your goons are likely to do? Threaten someone? Spark is really protective of the people he cares about, and you've already got Lucas beat up in the rec room. If one of your guys goes after

Greg, I'm not sure any of us is going to like what happens. It takes a lot to get Spark riled up but his temper is no joke. Things get really messy."

Lynn's sneer was shaky at best, but she wasn't going down easily. "We have plenty of shifters on our payroll. I'm sure they can handle one little mage and that blond brute."

"Blond brute?" Darien laughed out loud at that. "Oh, he's going to like that one. People usually get after him for being so pretty. *Brute.*" Darien snickered.

"That *brute* is one of the most powerful shifters around, and that *little mage* is the only vulcanmancer in North America," Caroline commented. "I'm pretty sure that they can handle your little shifters. Assuming that Spark doesn't call up another damned eruption because they went for Greg."

"I think he's the only one known in the western hemisphere, actually," Darien mused. His eyes had returned to their normal warm brown and he wasn't speaking with a lisp around his fangs anymore. "Mitch was on about it the other day when he was trying to get some information about something or other. Now then, Miss Graves."

Darien stepped over to her and held his hand out in silent demand.

Lynn snarled. "This is mine! I'm giving it to my lawyer! He'll get me out of this mess!"

Caroline cackled. "First, no court in the country would let someone into a courtroom with an actual weapon, let alone let them fondle the thing during a trial," she said. "Second, you and your cousin are going up on so many charges that I can't even think of them all, including trafficking in dangerous enchanted artifacts, assaulting Federal agents, kidnapping, and hiring hitmen. Oh, yeah, we found out about that. Third…" Caroline grinned now. "That's a fake anyway."

"What?" Darien cocked his head to the side and squinted at the thing.

"No!" Lynn denied. "No, I recognize it. I *know* this!"

"Yep. It *is* a pretty good replica. Spark found it in Lucas's bag just before you two dragged back to the room all bloody and injured." Caroline shrugged. "I don't think he ever meant to give you the real dagger, Lynn. Sorry. Lucas is a shady guy and is better at breaking into places than he probably should be, but he's got some pretty serious moral standards. Which I think you knew or you wouldn't have come at him with that entirely bogus story about being followed and trying to go to the FBI."

Lynn snarled, and in a last effort, used the dagger for its original purpose, stabbing out at Caroline. Darien was there, though, grabbing her wrist and twisting so that Lynn was on her knees in front of him, her hands both caught in his behind her back. The dagger skidded into a corner and lay there, useless to help anyone.

"More cuffs in my pocket, C. Then we're calling in some cars to haul off our latest crop of criminals," Darien said. "And then we're going to have another *long* chat about running headfirst into danger without any sort of plan and no backup."

Caroline dug into his pocket and pulled out the cuffs. "I had backup. You're here, aren't you?"

"Yes, we're here. Not that you actually arranged that, Caroline. I woke up when my damn phone went off for some reason, and then realized you were gone, and we had to follow the thread of the bloodbond I woke up with to find you since you had your phone turned off, and don't think we won't be discussing *those little tidbits, too*!" Darien was almost yelling by the time he finished talking. Rachel and Albert looked shocked and pale and flinched hard at the word "bloodbond," and Calder shrank back on the sofa as if he could hide in the overstuffed cushions.

Caroline sighed. "*I* set the alarm on your phone. I couldn't exactly take either you or Greg right away when I left because you both needed to rest up and heal a bit—you especially Mr. I-got-hit-with-a-*pipe*! And lord knows we've played this 'drink Caroline's blood, follow her all over everywhere' game before. I donated about half a glass to the cause and poured it down your throat because you didn't have any goddamn cans in your bag."

Apparently, Caroline was going to do a bit of yelling herself, because her volume was steadily rising. "And someone needed to stay there with you two boneheads in case you needed something. So I arranged it so you'd heal a bit faster *and* be able to track me down with plenty of time to spare, because I brought my go bag which has emergency supplies for just that sort of situation, once I calmed down for a second and thought enough to remember it. Lucas needs to get to a hospital *now*, D. He doesn't have your fancy paranormal healing abilities. I can't just dig out my emergency vampire first aid kit and heal *him*. And you want to talk about planning? *Let's talk about keeping your goddamn go bag stocked, shall we?*"

"Whoa, guys." Spark stepped into the room, wide-eyed. He was a bit rumpled but otherwise looked completely unscathed. "Everyone okay in here?"

Caroline glared at Darien who glared back.

"Okay." Spark stretched the word out for several seconds. "Well, Greg called in some locals to transport everyone, and they're sending an ambulance. He's staying with Lucas right now. I, um, I hope I didn't scare anyone too bad a little while ago. I sorta lost my temper a little when I saw him and I know there was some shaking. He's...it's really bad."

Caroline deflated. "Is he..."

"Greg's doing what he can. I guess he knows a lot of first aid," Spark said.

"He should. We all go through it, but he took extra classes and hangs out in the medical suite sometimes." Darien's concern bled through his words. Even Spark could probably hear it.

"Need any help with these–" Spark snarled. He had caught sight of Lynn. "*You?*"

There was a rumble that Caroline felt in her stomach more than anything else, and some of the decor rattled on the display shelves. Spark took a deep breath in through his nose and blew it out slowly. He repeated that a few times, and when Caroline glanced at Lynn she finally looked as worried as the rest of her allies.

"Spark, it's okay. We've got her, her weenie cousin Jeffy Junior, and their heavy hitter thugs. They're all going to go away for plenty of time to reflect on their poor life choices," Caroline said.

"Speaking of which. I'm curious about something, Sunshine." Darien's voice was much calmer now, and full of confusion.

"Yeah?"

"Why wasn't Miss Mage here able to flatten you? You're not magic-resistant."

Caroline felt like crowing but managed to put what she hoped was an earnest, professional expression on her face. She wasn't sure how successful she was when Spark started to snicker, but she rolled with it.

"I'm not magic-resistant," she said with a shrug. "But as we found out earlier, that sheath has a very serious suppressing enchantment that extends for a pretty significant bit away from the leather. So I stuck it in her belt loop when I pretended to stumble into her."

Darien's jaw dropped and Spark barked out a laugh which dissolved into a fit of cackles that he needed to sit down to slow.

"Oh my god, that's brilliant," he gasped at last. "You stuck her in a suppression bubble!"

"I thought you said you brought the fake," Darien said slowly.

"The fake *dagger*. Not the fake *sheath*." Caroline shrugged again, then let her grin creep over her face. There was a pounding on the front door and Spark jumped up.

"That's the paramedics. I didn't hear sirens, but I can sense the ambulance out there," he said. "I'll send Greg in here to help with cleanup once the medics have Lucas. I know you want to see him.

"Thanks, Spark," she said to his back as he hurried out.

"Well, Sunshine. Today has been one hell of a day."

"Wait till my lawyers finish with you!" Lynn managed to get her voice back now that Spark was out of the room.

"You have the right to remain silent too. I strongly suggest you don't give that up to issue threats," Caroline snarled back.

23

"I spend too much goddamn time sitting next to hospital beds," Caroline grumbled. Darien just answered with a small smile and handed her a cup of coffee from the shop down the street.

"Here. Spark made a food run. The stuff from the cafeteria was going to eat through your stomach," he said. "There's some sandwiches too."

"Thanks." She took a long sip of the coffee and sagged in the chair. Her mother had suggested that she go find the garden outside—there's always a garden outside a hospital, somewhere, she said—just to walk around in the sunshine for a few minutes. Caroline appreciated the advice since that was basically what she had called home for in the first place, but she didn't want to leave Lucas alone.

Mom hadn't been thrilled that one of her friends had been so badly hurt, and Caroline just knew that there was a lecture on dangerous jobs coming. When her parents realized that she wasn't just working at the FPAA as an intern, but with an eye to becoming an agent they became a lot more reserved in their support. They hated the idea of Caroline or any of her friends here being in danger, and neither of her parents was foolish enough to think that a career in the FPAA would be perfectly safe.

Filing and office work was one thing, but fieldwork was entirely another. Hence the last fourteen hours spent in the hospital waiting for Lucas to get through surgery to repair his badly broken left arm, and now for him to just wake up long enough to have a real conversation.

"He's going to be just fine, Sunshine," Darien reminded her. He pulled up a chair and plopped down into it. "The doctors are all very pleased with his progress."

"He's still out, though," she said.

"Well, he's on the good drugs. They'll be making him pretty sleepy." Darien reached out and rubbed her shoulder. He was an affectionate guy to begin with and it was always more pronounced when he was bloodbonded. It would wear off by the end of the week, she knew, but for right now she was damned glad of the comfort.

"But now that we know he'll be fine, and the dust is settling, you and I need to have a little chat. Point wants one as well, but is willing to wait a few days until Lucas wakes up and feels more comfortable," Darien said. Then after a pause, he continued with, "What, exactly, the hell were you thinking?"

Caroline could hear the anger in his voice, but under that she could hear the worry. The fear that she thought she was untouchable because of her luck in the past. Darien thought she was reckless and was afraid that her luck would eventually run out.

Caroline took a deep breath. "While you and Greg were out I got that video. I know we texted you that we'd gotten word from the kidnappers, but it was awful, D."

"I saw the photo and the video. That was smart to ask for, by the way," Darien said.

"Yeah, well," Caroline said. She swallowed to try to clear the lump in her throat as she looked at Lucas, small and almost fragile in the hospital bed, with his dark lashes brushing his cheeks. It just wasn't right to see him without that ever-present twinkle of mischief.

"Anyway, we were waiting for you. Because we are not stupid, you know." She turned back to Darien to meet his gaze. "I know that you and everyone else thinks that I run off without any plans or even thinking about things, but that's not true. We were waiting until you got back."

"And then we got back all beat up," Darien murmured.

"Yes, you incredible jerk!" Caroline griped. "Don't you dare get mad at me for not having a deep and involved planning session with your unconscious body."

Darien sighed and drove his fingers back through his hair, making it all stand on end. "I suppose that's fair."

"Greg was a bit better off than you were, but he still had a few wounds bad enough to make Spark nervous. So I decided to go ahead and let you come after me when you, at least, were up for it. I knew Greg would be okay, but Spark would be too distracted worrying about him to be any help if they didn't get at least a bit of rest."

"That's also true. It's pretty funny watching Spark get all protective." Darien's grin said it all. The pair of them were adorable together. Caroline wondered if Greg would ever get past his "I can only date manticores so I'll be alone forever" thing to see what was right in front of him. Then again, she wasn't sure she wanted to see Spark and Shakes fighting over him.

"So, I used my first aid kit and took enough of a blood sample to get you back on your feet without slowing me down and poured it down your throat from a cup so there was no risk of you accidentally taking too much. And while I gave that a chance to settle I dug out the fake dagger, stuck it in the real sheath, wrapped the whole thing in the suppressor cloth and stuck it in my bag. By then you had started to breathe more comfortably and were visibly healing faster, so I cut into my arm a bit and let you drink a mouthful or two right from the source to kick in the blood-bond so you could find me even if they managed to take my phone away, and I left the note with all the details. I'm still not clear on why fresh blood from a cup doesn't form a bond, but like, three drops from an arm does."

"I have no idea either." Darien slumped in his chair and dug his thumbs into the corners of his eyes. "You knew that I'd be awake and well enough to follow you inside of half an hour, so you guessed you only had that much of a head start."

"Yep," she said. "I figured in that it would take you maybe ten minutes to get Greg and Spark moving, so I figured I had forty-five minutes, tops, to get there, find out what I needed to know about where they had Lucas, and take out as many of them as I could on my own before you all showed up. I didn't expect Calder Junior to be there himself, and I definitely didn't expect to see Lynn. I am really not happy that she could talk her way around my weird ability."

"Yeah," he sighed.

"I asked her about that when she was taunting me." Lucas's voice was thin and rough, and he coughed hard as he croaked out the last word. Caroline was there in a flash with the cup of ice that was melting on the side table. Darien handed her a straw and a few minutes later, Lucas grunted that he was done. Caroline was about to jump into the questions that had piled up in her brain, but a nurse bustled in, asking Lucas questions and checking everything.

Finally, Caroline watched the nurse sweep out of the room promising the doctor's presence shortly, and she breathed a sigh of relief. So, it seemed, did Lucas, as his bed started raising up to let him sit.

"Show-off," she grumbled, but she could feel the relieved smile creeping onto her face.

"What's the damage?" Lucas asked, his voice still hoarse.

"Your left arm is a real mess. You needed surgery and now it has pins in it. You also have three cracked ribs and you're pretty much one giant bruise, with a few stitches thrown in here and there like sprinkles," Caroline told him. She knew she sounded just on the hysterical side of calm, but she was doing better since she had her sobbing fit while Lucas was in surgery. She glanced at Darien and couldn't even tell where she had snotted all over his shirt while she broke down. Actually, that might be a new shirt.

"You're on the good drugs, and they're going to keep you for a couple days, I think," she added.

Lucas just nodded.

"So tell us what happened, Lucas." Darien was a lot more rational in his question. Caroline had been about to go the *what the hell were you thinking* route, and suddenly she had a lot more sympathy for Darien. And Greg. And Point.

"I couldn't hear over you guys' chatting, and Lynn wasn't making much sense anyway. I just meant to step out of the room for a second. Just outside the door." Lucas sighed again. I started pacing while she talked and I guess I just started walking around the parking lot. You know, like I do sometimes when I'm thinking? I passed some trees and that's all I remember."

"They hit you with a tranq. Not elfshot, though," Darien told him. "Shakes caught it on one of the cameras."

"Ah." Lucas started to nod, but then winced. "Ugh. They had me in suppressing cuffs or I'd have sent an SOS with a location. They kept asking where the damn dagger was and why I hadn't turned it over yet. Lynn showed up with Junior practically on a leash. I'll give her this, she knows how to play people. Well, people she knows a bit. She thought she had my number, but I wasn't falling for it the way she thought I would."

"Yeah?" Caroline leaned forward. "How was that?"

"Well, first she thought she'd hook me the same way she hooked Calder." Lucas smirked at her. "I mean, she's attractive enough, sure, but I go for integrity and brains first. And feistiness."

"And that's why your grandfather is such a grumpy old man, hmm?" She smirked back. Somewhere behind her, Darien sighed.

"Anyway," he said, drawing the word out extra long. "She tried to use her feminine wiles on you and fell flat, hmm?"

"Yeah." Lucas shrugged. "What did work, though, and it worked on all of us, was appealing to our mostly law-respecting hero-ness. We wanted to help keep her safe from the big bad evil crime family cousin."

Caroline scrunched up her nose. "That's true. And I'm still pissed that I didn't hear her straight-up lying to our faces."

"Well, she explained that to me. It was a combination of a few charms and enchantments she had on her person and the fact that she didn't actually lie directly to us. She told us that she was close to her aunt, which was true. She told us that she was worried about how Jeff Calder Junior would do in charge, which was also true. She told us that she didn't meet up with an FBI agent. She did not, in fact meet up with one. She never planned to, but the near miss of the truth read more honest to you because of the enchantments. At least, according to her explanations."

"How did she know about my abilities, though?" If word was getting out, Caroline wasn't sure she was comfortable with the idea that criminals could see her coming.

"She didn't," Lucas said. He coughed again, and again Caroline helped him take a few sips of water. "Thanks. Anyway, she was assuming that you would try to use the dagger against her, and she was bragging that she had been finding ways around the thing for years. Basically, she wanted control of the family, and the best way to do that was to control Calder Junior and off Calder Senior. So she did. She *didn't* expect to have her aunt steal the dagger or for the thing to go missing for a year in which it became clear that allies and enemies alike had come to consider the damn thing a symbol of both the head of the Calder family and the source of their power. No dagger, no peaceful transition to the new leadership."

"So," Darien said with a frown. "She called you in a fake panic, drew you out, and kidnapped you. Why not just rush the motel room and take it?"

"She said that her security guy was very nervous of you two," Lucas said with a small grin. "Her plan was to get you guys alone, and then take you out, which she figured would leave Caroline and Spark vulnerable." He snickered and Darien unbent enough to chuckle along with.

"So when putting a hit out on us didn't get immediate results, she sent all her goons out to take down Darien and Greg," Caroline guessed.

"Pretty much, I guess." Lucas started to shrug but stopped with a groan. "Oh man. Everything hurts. And this bed sucks."

"I bet it does," Caroline said. "Just wait. My mom heard about you getting beat up and insisted that I bring you home with me this summer. I bet you'll wish you were right back here after a week of her fussing."

"Your mom wants me to visit?" Lucas's eyes got huge. "I'm going to meet your parents when I get out of here?

"Oh man, Lucas. She's probably halfway here already," Darien said, chuckling. "You're not going to know what hit you."

"Should I be scared? I'm kind of scared."

"Hey! That's my mom!" Caroline protested.

"You should be terrified," Darien said, laughing.

"Excuse me, Lucas, I need your pillow to smother a vamp."

Lucas started to laugh, then groaned in pain. "Stop being funny both of you. I'm wounded!"

Caroline glared at both the men in the room, but as soon as they stopped looking at her she sighed. Everything was going to be okay.

EXCEPT FROM PROPERLY PARANORMAL

The following is an unedited excerpt from Properly Paranormal, the second book in the Almost An Agent series

---

"So this goes way past any dinner party squabble, listen to this."

Lucas dashed in to Caroline's room with no other warning and plopped down on her bed, causing her to bounce.

"Is that Lucas? What's he on about?" Darien's voice held laughter, even through the phone. "What dinner party squabble?"

"Hang on, D. I'll put you on speaker. Now, start from the beginning, Lucas. I was barely through telling Darien about Cassie in the first place."

Lucas waved, as if she was on a video call, but kept his eyes on his tablet. That thing was probably so saturated in his magic that he probably didn't even need to look at the screen anymore. He could just let the information he wanted flow up his fingers while he held it.

"Hey, Darien. How's life? Okay, so. What Cassie told us was true, for the most part. Lacked a few details, but yes. The two men Miss Lawson's father approved of were at a dinner with the family and according to historical news articles, a disagreement arose and a fight broke out. But it wasn't between the two suitors. It was between the suitors and the father's secretary, a man named Albert Sowle. One of the men hit Sowle so hard that he stumbled back and hit his head on the mantle which knocked him out cold. He never woke up. I'd guess there were more injuries than just the head trauma, but the newspaper doesn't go into detail. If I am reading between the lines accurately, he was stabbed at least once."

"Yikes. Scandalous death of household staff," Darien said. "This was when, around the turn of the century?"

"1903, yeah," Lucas agreed.

"Wait. I thought that one of the approved suitors died?"

Lucas grinned over at her, his eyes sparkling. "They did. Eric Dixon, an up-and-coming owner of several factories, died several days later of injuries sustained in the brawl. Again the details are obscured, but it sounds like someone beat him up good. The other suitor up and left town the day after the fight."

Caroline scrunched her face up and thought about it. "So, the library is haunted by... the secretary? Albert Sowle?"

"There are a number of rumors and ghost-hunting sites that talk about the mansion, yeah. And they do speculate that Sowle is the cause of a number of unexplained phenomena. *But* they also speculate that the ghost is Zara Lawson herself."

"What's the logic there?" Darian asked.

Lucas' grin grew wider. "Pining for her lost love, and trying to find him."

"Oh no, the suitor that died was her lover and that's why she never married?" Caroline felt her heart squeeze. How tragic!

Lucas shook his head. "Nope. Sowle was. She tended to him personally, ordering a doctor in to dress the wounds and watching over him for the first day until she was too tired to stay awake. It sounds like dear old dad figured out that there was something going on between them and when Zara went to bed to rest for a bit, he had Sowle moved out of the house to a hospital of some sort, then refused to tell his daughter where her lover was. When word came of Sowle's death, Zara left the house that day and never returned until her father was dead. The ghost-hunting sites speculate that Zara Lawson haunts the halls of her home, waiting to be reunited with her—wait for it—her husband."

Lucas flipped the tablet around and Caroline saw a scan of an old marriage license. The couple listed were Zara Lawson and Albert Sowle, and it was signed by three witnesses whose names she couldn't begin to sort out. Lucas flicked a finger at the tablet and a fuzzy photograph of a couple gazing at each other appeared.

"This popped up when I searched for stories about the Lawson Library. One of the ghost sites admins tracked it down. They removed it from the site pretty quick, but there were comments and references to it already, so I dug into it, and voila." Lucas looked smug.

"Woah. That was a scandal." Darien said. "But..."

"Yeah. Ghosts don't actually exist, right?" Caroline asked.

WANT MORE?

Keep up with new releases, giveaways, and other antics by joining my email community. You'll get news of releases, a free short story, updates from any shenanigans I get up to, and all sorts of things!

ABOUT THE AUTHOR

Katherine Kim is a lifelong lover of fantasy. She started early, being read Tolkien as bedtime stories, which honestly explains a lot. More recently she's been drawn to more urban fantasy stories through both books and television, and reading continues to be a passion. She is an American that lives and writes in Tokyo, with her family.

If you liked this book, I hope that you'll leave me a review! I read every review and it makes a huge difference to me and to my work, but even just a few stars would make my day.

BOOKS BY KATHERINE KIM

Spirits of Los Gatos

Sarah's Inheritance

A Spirit's Kindred

Finding Insight

Brewing Trouble

Spiritkind

Federal Paranormal Activities Agency

Quick Study (Prequel)

Caroline's Internship

In The Blood

Heavy Traffic

Vampire's Curse

Fighting Fire

Almost an Agent

No Honor Among Thieves (this book!)

Properly Paranormal

Magaestra Trilogy

Magaestra: Found

Magaestra: Loyalties

Magaestra: Tested

Greenwoods Neighborhood

New to the Neighborhood

www.ingramcontent.com/pod-product-compliance
Lightning Source LLC
La Vergne TN
LVHW041810060526
838201LV00046B/1208